The Jerry McNeal Series

Village Shenanigans

(A Paranormal Snapshot)

By Sherry A. Burton

Also by Sherry A. Burton

The Orphan Train Saga
Discovery (book one)
Shameless (book two)
Treachery (book three)
Guardian (book four)
Loyal (book five)

Orphan Train Extras
Ezra's Story

Jerry McNeal Series
Always Faithful (book one)
Ghostly Guidance (book two)
Rambling Spirit (book three)
Chosen Path (book four)
Port Hope (book five)
Cold Case (book six)
Wicked Winds (book seven)
Mystic Angel (book eight)
Uncanny Coincidence (book nine)
Chesapeake Chaos (book ten)
Village Shenanigans (book eleven)
Special Delivery (book twelve)
Spirit of Deadwood (a full-length Jerry McNeal novel)

Clean and Cozy Jerry McNeal Series Collection (Compilations of the standalone Jerry McNeal series)

The Jerry McNeal Clean and Cozy Edition Volume one (books 1-3)

The Jerry McNeal Clean and Cozy Edition Volume two (books 4-6)

The Jerry McNeal Clean and Cozy Edition Volume three (books 7-9)

The Jerry McNeal Clean and Cozy Edition Volume four (books 10-12)

Romance Books (**not clean* - sex and language****)***

Tears of Betrayal

Love in the Bluegrass

Somewhere In My Dreams

The King of My Heart

Romance Books (*clean****)***

Seems Like Yesterday

"Whispers of the Past" (a short story)

Psychological Thriller

Surviving the Storm (Sex, Language, and Violence)

The Jerry McNeal Series

Village Shenanigans

By Sherry A. Burton

The Jerry McNeal Series: Village Shenanigans

By Sherry A. Burton
Published by Dorry Press
Edited and Formatted by BZHercules.com
Cover by Laura J. Prevost
@laurajprevostphotography
Proofread by Latisha Rich

For more information on the author and her works, please see www.SherryABurton.com

I will forever be grateful to my mom, who insisted the dog stay in the series.
To my hubby, thanks for helping me stay in the writing chair.
To my editor, Beth, for allowing me to keep my voice.
To Laura, for EVERYTHING you do to keep me current in both my covers and graphics.
To my beta readers for giving the books an early read.
To my proofreader, Latisha Rich, for the extra set of eyes.
To my fans, for the continued support.
Lastly, to my "writing voices," thank you for all the incredible ideas!

Chapter One

Of all the bad ideas Jerry had of late, spending the last few hours driving around in Jacksonville, North Carolina, visiting his old haunts may have been his worst. Instead of making him feel better, he was now feeling rather low, since, though he'd spent the better part of his Marine enlistment based at Camp Lejeune, there was nothing left for him here. Too much had changed since he'd left the area, and traffic, which had always been crazy, was now verging on insane. Sure, the new bypass helped, but the population had long outgrown the infrastructure of the roadways, and Jacksonville's traffic was what nightmares were made of.

Traffic flow aside, most of the Marines he'd served with had all either retired or moved on. The ones still on active duty were deployed elsewhere or had gone home for the holidays. He wasn't sure what he was expecting to find at his old stomping ground. Perhaps he'd hoped to run into some old friends who would give him an excuse not to follow through with his current plan of heading to his parents' house for the holidays. Not that he had a problem visiting his parents – it just wasn't home. His parents had sold his childhood home a few years ago and moved to The Villages, Florida. His grandmother's house – the one he'd spent most of his time when he was a child – had been sold after she passed. Jerry sighed. *Home*. He was driving his home. Everything he owned was crammed into bags in the back of his Durango, leaving him no place to truly call home. Jerry felt a tug in his heart.

Gunter pawed at Jerry's arm. Jerry reached a hand to pet his ghostly companion. "I'm alright, boy. Just feeling a bit melancholy."

Granny's voice sifted through the air. "How come I wasn't invited to your party?"

Jerry pulled his hand back and looked in the mirror to see Granny's spirit sitting in the back seat. "What party?"

Gunter disappeared. Instantly, he was in the back seat, whining and slathering Granny's spirit with ghostly kisses. Granny ruffled the dog's fur for several more seconds, then appeared in the front passenger seat. "Your pity party. You're not homesick, you know."

Jerry cocked an eyebrow. "I'm not?"

Granny lifted her feet to the dash. "No, you're lovesick."

Jerry slid a glance in her direction. "Since when did you become Dr. Phil?"

She ignored the quip. "I hate seeing you moping around like a lovesick puppy. You weren't happy when you lived here. What made you think you'd find happiness coming back?"

"I was happy."

Granny clicked her tongue. "You liked hanging out with your friends, but you weren't happy."

He started to argue with her but knew she'd see right through the ruse. They both knew he'd spent most of his adult life running from his gift. It wasn't until recently that he truly embraced it and found his calling by helping wayward spirits.

"You should have followed April and Max onto the plane."

Jerry could still see mother and daughter climbing the ladder to the Learjet and getting onto the plane. "I wasn't invited."

"You didn't ask," she reminded him.

Because April told me we don't have a future together. Jerry blocked the thought. "Granny, you're not helping."

"Oh poo, there I go meddling again." Granny reached into her pocket, pulled out an apple, rubbed it across the sleeve of her dress, and took a bite. "I have more. Want one?"

Not knowing where the apple came from, Jerry shook his head. "No, thank you. Listen, Granny, I know you mean well, but I don't think April feels the same way I do."

"Meaning you like her?"

I haven't stopped thinking about her since they left. "I care about both her and Max."

"Then why didn't you tell her?"

"Just because I care about them doesn't mean the feeling is mutual."

Granny huffed. "Of course they like you. Max thinks the sun rises and shines on you. She's a wonderful girl and extremely gifted."

Jerry readily agreed on that point. "I think Max is pretty cool too. But she's a kid, and kids are easy to impress."

Granny placed the half-eaten apple back in her pocket. "Yes, but Max told me her mom likes you."

She did? Not that it mattered what Max said; he'd heard the truth straight from April's mouth. "Max spoke out of turn. April told me there was no chemistry between us." There, he'd said it. Maybe now Granny would get off his back.

"Jerry Carter McNeal, you have a lot to learn about women!"

Gunter yawned a squeaky whine and promptly vanished.

Not for the first time, Jerry wished he could join him. "How's that?"

"Sometimes women say things to keep from getting hurt. April's been through a lot. She's not likely to put herself out there without knowing how you feel."

"What if I don't know how I feel? I mean, I like April, but you said it yourself, she's been through a lot. What if what I feel isn't enough?"

"Did you ever open the e-mail from Holly?"

Jerry shook his head. "No."

"Why not?"

Because I'm afraid to. "I haven't had the time."

"Uh-huh."

At long last, Jerry made it out of traffic and was able to increase his speed.

Granny placed her hand on his arm. "Not too fast, Jerry."

Jerry glanced at his grandmother. "I'm not even doing the speed limit."

"No, but I don't want you to miss anything."

"Like?"

"Not too much longer. You'll see him." Granny motioned down the road then disappeared.

Gunter appeared in the passenger seat the second she left. Jerry slid a glance in his direction. "Chicken."

Gunter smiled a K-9 smile.

"Granny said we're supposed to be watching for someone. Any clue who it is?"

Gunter licked his lips.

"Nope, don't think we're supposed to eat him."

Gunter snorted and placed his paws on the front dash.

Jerry's neck tingled as he surveyed the road ahead and saw someone walking on the side of the road. As he closed the distance, Jerry saw the person was carrying a seabag and noticed his hair was cut close to his head. "Looks to be a Marine."

The guy must have heard Jerry coming, as he turned and stuck out his thumb. Jerry looked at Gunter and sighed. "I hope Granny's right about this. The last time we picked up a hitchhiker, I nearly had to take a paternity test." Jerry made a mental note to call Seltzer and check in on Linda and the baby, and pulled to the side of the road.

The man started running. As he grew closer, Jerry motioned Gunter into the back seat and rolled down the window. As the guy stuck his head in the window, the hair on the back of Jerry's neck stood on end. He was no more than a kid and looked so young, Jerry doubted he'd even reached his twenty-first birthday. *Easy, Jerry, you're showing your age. He may be young, but it's obvious he's old enough to join the Marines.* Jerry eyed the guy. "How far are you heading?"

The Marine looked in the direction Jerry had just come from. "As far away as you can take me."

He's running. Not that it took psychic abilities to tell. Running was something Jerry was all too

Jerry looked in the review mirror, half expecting to see the dog rolling his eyes. "If I had a nickel for every time a recruiter promised something they couldn't deliver… Did you read your contract before you signed it?"

"Yeah."

"And it stated what you were and weren't getting?"

"I guess so. But the man promised me travel and adventure, and I'm stuck here in motor T. I go places alright, but all I do is drive in and around North Carolina. If all I wanted to do was drive a truck, I could have stayed home. There are plenty of truck-driving jobs there." Todd turned to face him. "My recruiter talked about all the fun places he'd visited and how he'd seen seven countries by the time he was twenty-one. There's nothing wrong with North Carolina, but the guy promised me the world, and I haven't been out of the state since I got here."

"Why not?"

Todd furrowed his brow. "What do you mean why not? I just told you they haven't sent me anywhere."

Jerry glanced at him. "Are you married?"

"No."

"You obviously don't own a car. If you did, you'd be driving it. Do you support your parents?"

Todd laughed. "No."

"Then what's stopping you from going places?

You got friends in Lejeune?"

Todd nodded. "A couple."

"You get thirty days' leave a year. What's stopping you from catching a mac flight to Naples, Germany, or Spain?"

"I guess I hadn't thought about it."

"You ever been to California?"

Todd shook his head.

"What's stopping you? Catch a flight and go to L.A. You can stay in the barracks for next to nothing, and they have people standing on the street giving away tickets to sit in the audience of game shows."

Todd's eyes were round, and Jerry could tell he was taking everything in. "You've done that?"

Jerry nodded. "Went out there with a couple of buddies. We got tickets to *The Price is Right*. My buddy even made it on stage. He didn't make it to the big showcase, but that's not the point. He won a theater system and got to spin the big wheel. It's not so big in person, by the way. My point is, you don't have to wait for anyone to send you where you want to go. Not that it matters, since you're heading home."

Todd turned away from him. "No, I'm not. I can't go home. Not yet anyway."

"Why not?" Jerry knew the answer but wanted to hear it from Todd.

"Come on, man, you know the reason. If I go

home now, everyone's going to know."

"Going to know what?" Jerry pressed.

"That I couldn't cut it as a Marine."

That was the comment Jerry had been waiting for. "Couldn't cut it? Did they kick you out?"

Todd sat up taller in his seat. "They didn't kick me out. I left."

"You mean you survived boot camp?"

"Survived? I got yelled at worse than that in high school. I aced boot camp. Except for the crucible; I thought I was going to die during that."

That was the fighting spirit Jerry had wanted to hear. "But you didn't, did you."

"No."

"Why not?"

Todd smirked. "No way I was going to let them get to me."

"Sounds like you are."

"Are what?"

"Letting someone get to you. You signed up for what, four years?"

"Yeah."

"Think about it, Dude. You are almost halfway through your enlistment. You should be able to do the other two standing on your head. Let me ask you, what made you want to become a Marine?"

"You mean besides the travel?" Todd laughed. "You wouldn't believe me if I told you."

Jerry slid a glance in his direction. "Try me."

"I was a wimp in school. When I told you I had it rough, I wasn't lying. Anyway, there were all these jocks, and they always got the girls. Then we had a Marine recruiter show up on Career Day. He came in wearing his Marine uniform, and all the girls in class were practically drooling over the guy. I didn't see anything special. It wasn't like he had movie star looks. But it didn't seem to matter because he had that uniform. I heard the girls whispering – saying how the uniform made him so hot, and it got me thinking. I knew I wouldn't ever be a jock, but nothing was stopping me from being a Marine."

Jerry glanced at Todd. "Doesn't sound like there's much stopping you from walking away either."

Todd sighed, and Jerry knew he was getting to him. "Todd, let me ask you a question. Where are all those jocks that used to give you crap when you were in school?"

"I guess they are still living in our same hometown. I didn't keep track of them, but I suppose most of them are still there."

"And what about you, Todd? What did you do?"

"I joined the Marines."

"And you're willing to throw all that away just because you haven't booked yourself a vacation?"

"I guess it does sound kind of stupid when you put it like that." Todd sighed and ran a hand over his head.

"What if no one picks me up?"

Jerry smiled. "They won't have to. I'm taking you back myself."

"Why would you do that?"

Jerry smiled. "Because I'm a Marine, and that's what Marines do. We take care of our brothers."

Chapter Two

If not for the fact he'd promised to take the kid back to the barracks, Jerry would have dropped him off on the outskirts of town. As it was, Jerry had decided to go back to Jacksonville to grab a bite to eat. He took a left onto Western Boulevard and once again found himself fighting traffic. The dash lit up, showing a call from Seltzer. Jerry answered.

"Jerry, my boy, where are you?"

"Sitting in traffic in Jacksonville, North Carolina."

"Bet you miss your lights and siren."

"You can say that again. Fred promised if I'm a good boy, he'll authorize me a set." Actually, Fred had already promised to get the system installed as soon as Jerry found time to be without his vehicle for any length of time, not an easy feat when Jerry practically lived in the thing.

"How's that going?"

Jerry laughed. "What? Being good or working for Fred?"

"Both."

"Good, actually. Fred is a lot like you before you got your hands tied." Jerry knew Seltzer was a bit jealous of his new boss and hoped the comment would appease the man.

"I'm glad you can finally use that gift of yours like it was intended. So, what kind of ghostly case has you in Jacksonville?"

"More of a ghost from my past." Jerry went on to tell Seltzer about Todd and his decision to bring him back. "Granny is the one who told me to watch for him. I guess she felt the connection as well."

"So what you're telling me is that the ghost of your dead grandmother points you in the right direction?"

"Pretty much. It's not the first time and probably won't be the last. Although I was a bit apprehensive about picking up another hitchhiker this soon after Linda. How is the mother-to-be anyhow? Still living in your spare room?"

"She is. I'm not sure how much longer she'll be here, though."

Jerry felt his jaw twitch. "Don't tell me she's going back to her loser boyfriend."

"Nope, she's over Sean. She has a new squeeze."

"That didn't take long. Anyone I know?"

"Manning."

"Manning!? How did those two meet?" Jerry's laughter was met with a growl. Apparently, the K-9 didn't like Jerry disrespecting his former handler. Jerry looked over at Gunter and mouthed the word "sorry."

"How do you think they met?"

Jerry smiled. "If I had to guess, I would say June." Most of the troopers at the state police post where he used to work knew Seltzer's wife for her match-making antics. What wasn't common knowledge was the police sergeant's wife made a living writing smutty police romance and enjoyed seeing her books come to life. "Let me guess, she's trying to get fodder for her next novel."

"Come on, McNeal, I thought we were friends. Why'd you have to go putting that image in my head?"

Jerry shook off his own image. "So, Manning doesn't have a problem with Linda being pregnant?"

Seltzer chuckled. "Apparently, you don't remember how lazy Manning is. The guy's probably thrilled someone else did the work for him."

Jerry laughed. Gunter growled a deep growl, and Jerry resisted a witty comeback. Plus, if he had to be honest with himself, he envied the guy – not that Manning was with Linda; it was more that Manning had found someone who made him happy.

"You still with me, McNeal, or did I lose you?"

"I'm still here."

"I almost forgot. The reason I called is June wanted me to ask if you'd come for Thanksgiving dinner."

"Why? Who needs a date?"

Laughter drifted through the dashboard. "No one. At least, not that I'm aware of. You know she likes to have family around her during the holidays."

Jerry wasn't family, not by blood anyway, but at one point, Jerry had felt closer to Brian Seltzer and his wife June than he had to his own parents. "Sorry, no can do this year. I already have plans."

"Anything good?"

"The jury's still out on that. I'm going to spend time with my parents."

"You don't sound too happy about it. I know you and your parents have had your struggles, but I thought you'd moved past that in recent months."

"We have. At least, I hope so. It just feels weird going to Florida for the holidays. I don't mind Florida. It's just nothing will feel familiar." Jerry sighed. "I guess I'm just a bit homesick for a home I don't have."

"You know you always have a place at our table," Seltzer reminded him. "But I get the feeling there's more to it than that. I've got a good shoulder, you know."

Jerry drummed his fingers on the steering wheel, debating, then finally asked what was on his mind.

"How did you know June was the one?"

"Because I couldn't quit thinking about her. Does this have something to do with that woman who called here asking for your information?"

Jerry sighed. "I don't know."

"Son, talking to you is like sitting in my boat waiting for the fish to bite. If you have something on your mind, just say it, and I'll give you the benefit of my years of expertise."

The light turned green.

Jerry followed several cars through the intersection before stopping at the next light. "What's on my mind is Max's mom, April. I thought maybe she felt something too, but then she told me we didn't have any chemistry."

"That had to smart. What'd you say in return?"

"Nothing, and the next day, I watched her get on the plane to head home."

"Want June to call her? She's pretty good at that matchmaker stuff, you know?"

"No." The word came out louder than he'd planned. Jerry took a breath. "Please don't tell June."

"I won't, but just know she'd jump right in with both feet if she knew about this."

"I know. I'm just not sure I'm ready for her help. I need some more time to think things through."

Traffic started moving again. Jerry eased off the brake, made his way through the intersection, and kept going when the next light remained green. A car pulled out into traffic from the right, and the vehicle in front of him slowed. Jerry slowed and jerked forward as his Durango slid sideways into the next lane. Coming to a stop, he looked in the mirror and sighed as Gunter placed his feet on the center console, barking his discontent.

Jerry sighed. "No good deed goes unpunished."

"Problem."

"Just got tagged. I'd better go see how bad it is." Jerry ended the call, and Gunter followed him out of the Durango.

The man in the Ford F150, behind him for the last thirty minutes, met him at the back of the Durango. "What the Sam Hill were you doing stopping like that?" the guy asked heatedly.

Jerry let out a long breath. "As a rule, if the person in front of you stops, that means you should too."

Gunter moved in between the two and stood watch over the other driver as Jerry turned to assess the damage. His heart sank – the bumper was crumpled beyond repair, and both taillights were busted. Though technically drivable, he would be pulled over by every cop he passed. While Jerry wasn't a mechanic, he knew it would take more than a few days in the shop, and that was providing they had the parts and paint on hand. Jerry turned to face the guy and saw the man had his cell phone out recording him. Jerry nodded to the CVS parking lot. "Let's move to the parking lot and exchange information."

"Yeah, I leave, and you tell the cops it's my fault."

Jerry sighed. "You do realize you're the one who hit me, right?"

"Only because you slammed on your brakes in front of me."

Jerry looked at the traffic, which was growing worse by the moment. "Move your truck to the parking lot."

"No way, man. I'm not going anywhere until the cops arrive."

Jerry looked at Gunter. It was so very tempting to give the dog the okay to bite the man. Instead, he pulled out the gold badge Fred had given him and held it up for the guy to see.

The man's eyes grew wide, and he lowered the cell phone. "Why didn't you say you were a cop?"

Fred was right – this thing does come in handy. Jerry pocketed the badge. "Guess I was just waiting to see if we could handle this like gentlemen." Jerry walked to his Durango without another word. As soon as he was inside, he called 911 and reported the accident. The man who had hit him followed him into the lot but made no move to exit his vehicle. It was just as well as Jerry didn't want to fabricate another lie as to why they needed to wait for the real police.

***

Gunter was lying in the backseat gnawing on a bloody bone when the officer arrived. Though Jerry got out, Gunter did not. Jerry leaned against his driver's side door, waiting for the officer to approach. It didn't take long.

Officer Lewis approached from the driver's side, keeping his right hand free. Jerry handed the officer his license and registration. He took it and leveled a look at Jerry. "The gentleman in the other vehicle said you claimed to be a cop."

Jerry shook his head. "Nope, just showed him my badge."

Lewis rocked back on his heels. "How about you show it to me? Real easy like."

Jerry thought to tell the man he'd left his gun in the Durango but knew better than to mention the word gun when the officer was already on the defensive. He held up his left hand and moved his right hand to his front pocket, carefully withdrawing his gold badge and showing it to Lewis.

Lewis arched an eyebrow. "Lead Paranormal Investigator. Is this a joke?"

Jerry smiled. "That's what I asked when they gave it to me."

"You're not trying to get smart with me, are you?"

"No, sir. I've been in law enforcement long

enough to know better than that. I was a state trooper for a number of years," Jerry added to clarify.

"North Carolina?"

Jerry shook his head. "Pennsylvania."

The officer didn't look impressed. Then again, that could be because Gunter had materialized and was currently sniffing the officer's crotch. Lewis shifted against the unseen intrusion to his manly bits and frowned. "While I'd like to take you at your word, I'm still going to have to run you."

Jerry had been expecting this. "I'd do the same thing in your shoes."

The officer took Jerry's information back to his cruiser. Gunter sat and scratched an imaginary itch. Three minutes later, Jerry's cell rang. Jerry looked at the caller ID and smiled as he pressed to connect. "That didn't take long."

"What'd you get stopped for?"

"I didn't. I called them."

"Trouble?"

"Some jerk rear-ended me." Jerry sighed. "It's smashed up, but nothing a good body shop can't fix."

"Really? Where are you?"

"Jacksonville."

"Fantastic."

Jerry laughed. "You don't have to sound so excited about it."

"Don't you see this is perfect? You get yourself

a rental car, and I'll send someone to pick yours up. While it is in the shop, we'll install the lights, sirens, and a few other treats."

"Don't bother with the treats. Gunter doesn't eat them."

Gunter stopped scratching at the mention of his name. The dog got up and walked toward the truck that rear-ended him.

"That's not the kind of treat I was referring to," Fred said dryly.

Jerry watched as Gunter appeared inside the cab of the truck. Almost immediately, the man started waving his hands in the air. "So what are we talking? James Bond stuff?"

Fred chuckled. "Hardly. I was thinking of a few more electronics and, say, a computer system. In your line of work, I think we should add a tracking device. Call and have the rental company pick you up. Text me your location, and I'll send someone for your ride."

Jerry started to accuse Fred of wanting to keep tabs on him, then realized he didn't need a tracking device to accomplish that – a point that had been proven when they had needed to find Doc. At the thought of his friend, Jerry sighed. "Do whatever you have to do."

The driver of the truck opened the door and scrambled out, still waving his hands in the air.

Jerry walked to the back of his Durango.

"Problem?"

The man frowned. "Dang no-see-ums; the truck seems to be full of them."

The man was talking about tiny flies – pesky and nearly invisible, they were a common irritant in the south. Though Jerry knew the man's problem wasn't flies, pesky and invisible did well to sum up his problem as Gunter now sat in the driver's seat of the man's truck, staring out over the steering wheel. Jerry turned so the man couldn't see his smile.

Chapter Three

Though it only took twenty minutes for a flatbed to arrive to pick up the Durango, it took three phone calls to find a rental agency able to pick him up. Jerry looked at the yellow arches in the next parking lot, then looked at his bags and sighed. "Yo, dog. Keep an eye on my bags. I'm going to run next door and grab a sandwich."

Gunter barked, then disappeared, reappearing several seconds later wearing his K-9 police vest to let Jerry know he'd understood.

Jerry started to leave, then reconsidered. He returned and picked up his gun bag. "Nothing personal, dog."

Gunter growled.

Jerry ordered a couple of burgers, fries, and a tea and then ordered a cup of ice cream to appease Gunter. Exiting the building, he saw a man walking toward his bags. Dressed in baggy jeans that looked as if they needed a belt and a white t-shirt, the man kept looking over his shoulder as if checking to see if he was being watched. Jerry smiled. *This ought to be good.*

The man saw Jerry coming and hurried to the bags.

Jerry stopped three feet away. "You wouldn't be trying to steal my bags, now would you?"

The man swallowed. His Adam's apple bobbed in his throat. "What do you mean your bags? I left these here when I went inside to buy a pack of smokes."

"Is that so? How about you try to pick them up."

The guy bent to pick up Jerry's bags, and Gunter took his hand in his mouth. The man's eyes grew wide as he jerked his hand free. "What was that?"

Jerry shrugged. "What was what?"

The guy scratched his head as he reached for the bags once more. Once again, Gunter grabbed the man's hand in his teeth. The man sucked in his breath, pulled his hand back, and turned it back and forth in front of his face. He looked at Jerry. "You seeing this?"

Jerry shook his head. "All I see is some clown trying to take something that doesn't belong to him."

The man narrowed his eyes and tugged at his jeans. "Who you calling a clown?"

Jerry smiled. "There are only two of us here, and

I'm not the one acting funny."

"Yeah, we'll see who's funny." The man doubled his fist. As he stepped forward, Gunter jumped up, placing his paws on the guy's chest. The man's face paled. "What the heck, man? It's like you have a force field around you."

Jerry leaned forward and lowered his voice. "It's something new the government is working on. The black helicopters will be here soon. You can't see them on account of they are in stealth mode. They find out you've been messing with me, and they'll be on you."

Gunter lowered to the ground. The guy held up his hands. "I wasn't messing with you. I thought those were my bags. Turns out my bags are on the other side of the building." He started to turn and stopped. "You radio those copters and tell them I didn't mean any harm. You hear?"

Jerry looked to the sky. "You get out of here now, and I won't even tell them your name." The guy took off running. Jerry looked at Gunter and smiled. "How long do you think it'll be before he realizes I don't know his name?"

Gunter barked and wagged his tail. The next time Jerry looked, Gunter wasn't wearing his vest.

Jerry lowered to the sidewalk and set out the cup of ice cream for Gunter. As Jerry ate his meal, Gunter chased after the cup with his tongue. They'd both just finished eating when a horn blared. Gunter moved in front of Jerry and barked.

Jerry looked to see a small turquoise car speeding into the parking lot. The car cut the corner and veered straight toward him. Just when Jerry wondered if the guy was going to plow into them, the vehicle swerved and slid to a stop sideways in front of him.

Dressed in a suit that looked to be a size too big and driving a car that was three sizes too small, the driver reached across the seat and lowered the passenger window. "You McNeal?"

Jerry winced as he rose from the sidewalk. "Yep."

The guy reached around the front seat and unlocked the passenger side door. "Put your stuff in the back."

Jerry looked toward his bags and sighed. "I've got a couple cracked ribs. Can I get some help with my bags?"

The man bobbed his head, then put the car into park. He got out, walked around the car, and reached through the window to unlock the back door. After folding down the seat, he grabbed Jerry's bags, placing them inside. He looked at Jerry. "Name's Eric. Do you need help getting in?"

Jerry waved him off. "No, I can manage on my own." Jerry looked at Gunter, who was eyeing the car as if to say, *I'm not getting in there, and you can't make me.* As if to prove his point, the dog disappeared.

Eric hurried to the driver's side and opened the door. "Okay, let's roll. Traffic is beyond brutal out there. We've had several units return from overseas in the last two days – bad for traffic and good for business."

Eric got in, slammed his door shut, and tore off out of the parking lot even before Jerry had buckled his seatbelt. Eric turned his head to Jerry. "So, what's your story? How'd you wind up stranded in the CVS parking lot?"

"Got rear-ended. They picked up my Durango about twenty minutes ago." Jerry looked for the button to power up his window and saw there wasn't one. He cranked the handle, remembering how many times he'd done the same in the old truck he'd inherited from Granny. Only this wasn't an old truck. It was a car, a new one at that. *Must be the stripped-down version.*

"Sucks you got hit, but you're lucky they picked it up so fast. I guess that means you'll be needing a car for a few months. I hope you have good insurance. It'll take at least that long. The shops around here have a waiting list months out."

Good thing Fred has hookups. "I'll be taking the car to Florida."

Eric frowned. Before he could say what was on his mind, he smiled and pointed. "Check it out, Jacksonville's own superhero is back on the corner."

Jerry looked out the window to see a man wearing camo pants kicking his leg up in the air. Sweat glistened off his ebony torso as he twisted and turned, doing one karate move after the other. The man's chiseled physique and ease of movement belied his age. Jerry smiled. "The Jacksonville Ninja."

Eric bobbed his head. "You've heard of him, then? His name's Radio, least that's what he tells people."

"Yep. He was a staple on the corner when I was stationed here."

"Man, I hope I can move like that when I'm sixty." The light turned green. Eric pressed the gas, zipping into the intersection. "When were you here?"

"2010 to 2015. So much has changed, and yet in some ways, it's like I never left. It's busier, and there are new roads to navigate, but the endless rows of tattoo parlors and barbershops are still a staple. I drove past Gus's Warehouse and about threw up just thinking about the last time I was there."

Eric laughed. "Must have been a Wednesday."

Jerry nodded. "I see I'm not the only one familiar with nickel draft night. I don't think I've touched a PBR since I left Jacksonville. Between Gus's, Tobies and Driftwood, they tell me I had a real good time while I was here."

"Driftwood, there's a blast from the past. It's the

Platinum Gentlemen's Club now. The girls are HOT!" Eric whipped the wheel, cutting into the other lane. The Spark jutted forward as they passed two cars and zipped back into the lane they'd just left.

The guy drives like a maniac. I've lived through wars, and now I'm going to die in a teal-blue roller skate. Jerry looked for something to hold on to and found nothing, so he stretched his legs, bracing himself for the accident he was sure to come. Somehow, he didn't think the car would fare well if they did. On the one hand, Jerry wanted to tell the guy he was going to have him arrested for reckless driving. On the other, he was glad Eric was speeding, as it meant the ride would be finished sooner.

Eric cut across traffic, zoomed into the rental car lot, and put the car into park.

As he got out, Jerry opened the door and surveyed the empty parking lot. He looked over the roof of the car at Eric. "Tell me you keep the inventory on another lot."

Eric smiled a sheepish grin. "Nope."

"So, I'm not getting a rental?"

"Sure you are." Eric's gaze darted toward the shoebox they'd just crawled out of. "And you don't even have to transfer your bags. I know what you're thinking. But I can assure you that you won't find another rental in this town tonight. You're welcome to try, but if someone calls before you agree to this one, you'll lose it too."

Jerry eyed the man. "You trying to pull a fast one, Eric?"

"No, just telling you like it is. I would hate to see you having to walk, with your ribs hurting and all."

***

Gunter appeared in the passenger seat, did a tight circle, and lowered with a groan.

"I don't want to hear it. You haven't been locked up inside this thing for the last five hours!"

Gunter yawned, and Jerry sighed. "I'm sorry I yelled. It's not the car so much as the fact that everything I own fits inside. Pretty pathetic, don't you think?"

Gunter placed his head on the console and looked at Jerry with soft brown eyes.

Jerry fished out his cell phone, found Fred's number, and hit dial. He held it to his ear and waited.

"McNeal? I didn't expect to hear from you so soon. Anything wrong?"

"I want my Durango back." Jerry suddenly felt like a kid begging for a favorite toy.

"Sorry, no can do. It's already loaded onto a truck heading to the compound. Is there a problem with your rental?"

Jerry blew out a sigh. "The problem is they forgot to give me the rest of it."

"What the heck did you get?"

"A Chevy Spark. I feel like I'm driving a roller skate. I have semis passing me, and I'm afraid I'm going to get blown away by their backdraft." Jerry heard Granny's voice sing-song in his mind. *Quit being so dramatic, Jerry.* Of course, she was in his mind. There was no place for her to sit.

"My aunt drives a Spark. She seems to like it well enough."

"Here's the thing about Marines, Fred. They don't drive well enough – they drive fine. A Marine either drives a fine ride or they walk." He instantly thought of Todd and wondered how he'd fared with his sergeant.

"So why'd you choose it? Jacksonville is a fairly big town. Are you telling me they didn't have anything else?"

"I guess they had a few units come in today, and everything was cleaned out. It also explains why traffic is even worse than I remember. I remember how it was back in the day – guys got back and spread out like locusts. It didn't matter we'd been gone for months on end; we were always eager to go someplace. The ones who didn't have rides rented them, and I guarantee no Marine walked onto a rental lot and said give me the smallest ride you've got. The guy at the lot said he could get me something tomorrow, but I figured if the cars were gone, there probably wouldn't be any hotel rooms either. Hey, do me a favor."

"What's that?"

"If I have an accident, change the accident report to say I was killed jumping out of a helicopter or something."

Fred laughed. "You think I can do that?"

Jerry held the phone out and looked at it. "Yes."

Another laugh. "You're right, I can. Don't worry, McNeal, if you die on your way to your parents' house, I'll make your death sound real cool. Why, it'll be so cool, every newspaper in the country will pick it up. How does that sound?"

Jerry smiled. "It sounds as if you are pacifying me. And, Fred?"

"Yeah, McNeal?"

"If you are, I'm going to come back and haunt you, and you know I can do it." Jerry looked at Gunter. The dog smiled.

"You good, McNeal?" Fred's words drifted through the phone, and instantly, Jerry thought of Doc.

Golden. Jerry rolled his neck and resisted saying the phrase he'd used with Doc and the others from his unit. "I'm good. Hey, while I have you on the phone, I was wondering if you've heard any news about Doc."

"No. Do you want me to reach out?"

Jerry sighed. "Nah, I was just wondering if you heard anything. He'll be in touch when he's able."

"Safe travels, and, McNeal, don't get dead."

"Hadn't planned on it." The screen flashed, letting Jerry know Fred had ended the call. While the man wasn't Doc, their conversation had worked to calm him. As he drove, his mind drifted back to Doc. *I hope you're doing okay, Doc.* Jerry had often been called a hero, something that embarrassed him each time it happened. He'd merely gone where he was told and done what he'd been trained to do. While his gift had often alerted him to trouble, there was little he could do to shut it down. Doc, on the other hand, was a true hero. The man had carried the weight of the world on his shoulders for so many years without complaint: heading out with the Marines and staying low as the battle raged all around, biding time waiting for someone to yell Corpsman up, then running into the fray and fighting to save a life in the worst of conditions. Something like that had to take its toll on a man.

A stench filled the air, drawing him out of his musings. Jerry glanced at Gunter. "Did you do that?"

Gunter smiled a K-9 smile.

Chapter Four

It took just over ten hours for Jerry to drive to his parents' home in the Rio Ponderosa section of The Villages. The houses sat right next to each other – each nearly identical with front-facing garages and small white picket fencing. The only thing that kept the homes from looking exactly alike was the siding color and varied landscape. His parents' two-bedroom, two-bath home had white siding and sat on a quiet road that backed to a swamp.

Jerry pulled into the driveway and let out a heavy sigh. Gunter seemed to be just as happy to be out of the tiny space, spinning in circles as Jerry unfolded himself from the car. Jerry approached the house and smiled. Within the graveled landscaping were frogs of all shapes and sizes. His mother loved frogs and had collected them for years. When searching for the perfect home within the Villages, the realtor had tried to steer his parents toward one of the newer communities, even suggesting they consider a new build; however, as soon as his mother learned of one for sale near the swamp, she knew that was the one she wanted.

Lori didn't care about the mosquitoes or the fact that they would be living in an older neighborhood. Her only thought was to sit on her small screened-in patio and listen to the frogs sing from the edges of the swamp. His father Wayne was happy to accommodate her, as living in an older home meant saving money, since the house's yearly bond, which went toward the community's infrastructure, was already paid off. While his father would have agreed to purchase a newer home, he was just as happy not to have the added cost.

Jerry stepped up to the door, pressed the doorbell, and waited. Gunter wasn't as patient. He slipped through the closed door without waiting for an invite. Not for the first time, Jerry questioned his decision to show up to his parents' home unannounced. *Way to go, McNeal. They're probably not even home.* He laughed. *Heck, they're probably not even in the state. It's the holidays. They most likely went to Tennessee to spend Thanksgiving with Uncle Marvin and his family.* Then again, he hadn't seen anything about their leaving on Facebook, and his mother put everything on there. Jerry scratched his head and rang the doorbell once more. *You're wasting your time, McNeal. The house is not that big. If they were home, they would have answered by now. It'll serve you right if you drove the shoe box here for nothing, all because you were too stubborn to give your mother a courtesy call to let her know you were coming.*

Gunter stuck his head out the door.

Jerry sighed. "I don't suppose you could unlock the door for me?"

Gunter answered by pushing the rest of his body outside.

"Maybe they keep a key hidden among the frogs." Jerry looked under the doormat and then moved around the gravel, lifting the green statues. Having no luck, he walked to the back of the house and tried the screen door. Locked. *Give it up, McNeal. Unless you're willing to break in or leave without them ever knowing you were here, you will have to call.* Jerry mulled over his options, deciding he'd call and ask where they were. If he found they had taken off for the holidays, he would leave and never let them know he'd been there.

A bullfrog croaked nearby, and Gunter headed toward the sound.

Jerry heard a splash. *Great, the dang dog is going to get eaten by an alligator.* Jerry started after him.

"Don't take another step, or I'll shoot!" Though the woman's voice sounded firm, Jerry felt a whirl of fear and uncertainty surrounding her.

Jerry froze.

"Now, put your hands up."

Gunter, if you're finished chasing bullfrogs, I could use some help. Jerry lifted his hands and heard a gasp. Instantly, he knew the person behind him had seen the pistol sticking out of his waistband. *Crap.*

"Now, what do I do?" The woman's voice lowered to a whisper as if she were talking to someone. "Maybe I should make him lie on his belly. No? Oh yes, that is much better." She firmed her decision. "Interlock your hands and place them on the back of your head. Oh, yes, you were right, that is much better."

As Jerry placed his hands on his head, he suddenly felt like he was in an episode of *Murder She Wrote*. He decided to try to reason with the woman. "I'm not trying to rob the place. My parents live here."

"Oh yeah? What are their names?"

"Wayne and Lori McNeal." As Jerry spoke, he slowly turned to face the woman. She was tall and slender with short, silver hair and wore a pale yellow pant set with leaves embroidered on the shirt. He tried to see who she was speaking to, but she was too quick, pointing the flashlight to his eyes as if purposely trying to blind him. He squinted and saw a pistol in her left hand. "Mind lowering that thing?"

"He does look a lot like Wayne," the woman whispered.

"That's because I'm his son," Jerry assured her.

She leveled the gun at him. "What's your name?"

"Jerry, Jerry McNeal," he added, putting emphasis on the last name. "Please stop pointing that gun at me. It's likely to go off."

The woman lowered the flashlight but kept the gun trained on him. She smiled. "Honey, I've handled guns all my life and have never had one go off unless I wanted it to. I don't aim to shoot you unless you give me a reason to."

Jerry felt the truth in her words and relaxed ever so slightly.

Another light floated through the darkness. The woman kept the gun aimed at him and turned her light on the newcomer.

A blonde lady wearing a pink housecoat and slippers and wielding an oversized umbrella stepped up beside the woman. "Gertie? I saw the light. What's going on?"

"I saw this man pull in. At first, I thought it was Lori and Wayne, but the car was too small. This guy got out and tried the door. When no one answered, he started snooping around, so I got my gun. He claims his parents live here. Says his name is…"

The newcomer cut Gertie off. "Jerry?"

Jerry wasn't sure who the woman was but was glad the lady knew his name. "That's right. Now if we can stop pointing the gun."

"Put that thing away," the woman who'd just

arrived hissed. “This is Jerry. You know …Jerry.”

Gertie gasped and lowered her pistol. “The one with the dog?”

Jerry’s mouth went dry. *They know about Gunter. How?*

Gertie frowned. “I thought he drove an SUV. That thing is no bigger than my golf cart, and I know it doesn’t have a hemi. I know what that motor sounds like. If you ask me, it sounds like his old man’s been stretching the truth. Besides, if the guy was as good as Wayne said, he would never have let us sneak up on him. Isn’t that right, Herbert?”

Jerry wasn’t sure who Herbert was, but Gertie was right; he’d been so worried about Gunter taking a swim in the swamp that he’d been caught off guard. That the dog had yet to show up was even more concerning than the fact that his father had told people about Gunter. Jerry squinted to see through the dark but didn’t see anyone else standing beside the woman.

Gertie heaved an exaggerated sigh. “I hope that doesn’t mean he was lying about the dog and what else the boy can do.”

The woman in the robe grabbed Gertie’s hand and moved the flashlight around. “Jerry, is the dog here?”

Jerry started to tell them there wasn’t a dog but thought of his father’s credibility and decided against it. “No, ma’am, not at the moment. I’m afraid you have me at a disadvantage. I didn't get your names."

"Sandy Cottingsworth, and Annie Oakley here is Gertie Martin. We are your parents' neighbors. Now, I can understand Gertie not knowing you were coming. She lives on the other side of the road. But me, why, I live right next door. I talk to Wayne and Lori every day. I'm surprised they didn't tell me you were coming." Her tone left no doubt her feelings were hurt by the exclusion.

Jerry smiled a sheepish smile. "I'm sure they would have told you if they'd known."

Both women gasped, showing him he'd committed a mortal sin. It was Gertie who called him on it. "Bless your heart. For someone who's supposed to know things, you don't seem very bright."

Having been raised in the south, Jerry knew the comment to be a dig even before she accused him of not being very bright. Jerry pulled himself taller, searching his mind for a proper comeback. Thinking of his grandmother, he hung his head, pretending to regret his decision to come, which wasn't a total farce. "Yes, ma'am, I am quickly coming to see the error of my ways."

Sandy clicked her tongue. "Gertie's right, Jerry. You should have called. Your momma's going to be beside herself."

"Our family is not into formalities. Someone

shows up at the door, you let them in, simple as that."

Gertie waved the flashlight at him. "You mark my words, your momma might say she doesn't mind, but all the while, she's going through the list of things she has to do to make you comfortable."

Sandy nodded. "You are so right, Gertie. Why, I have half a mind to use my key and go in and start tidying up for her."

Jerry raised an eyebrow. "You have a key to my parents' house?"

Sandy smirked. "Of course. We exchanged keys right after they moved in."

Gertie snickered. "You better explain yourself, or you're going to give Jerry the wrong idea."

Sandy elbowed her. "I didn't mean it like that, and Jerry knows it."

"I'm not sure I understand anything at the moment." Jerry smacked at a mosquito. "What am I missing?"

Gertie spoke up. "Oh, you must not have googled The Villages when your parents decided to move here. On the other hand, I did a lot of research before moving. There are some that think the bubble is nothing but sex and drugs and old people transmitting disease."

Jerry cringed and swatted another mosquito. "The bubble?"

Sandy smiled. "You really don't know much, do

you – 'bout The Villages, that is. The bubble is how people refer to The Villages. Honestly, I've been a little disappointed that I haven't been invited to a swingers' party."

Gertie snickered once more. "Me too. The closest I've come is getting hit on by Mr. Dunlap down at the pool."

Sandy joined Gertie in her giggles. "Of course, Mr. Dunlap isn't his real name. She just calls him that because his belly has done lapped over his trunks."

Jerry felt Gunter appear. The dog waited until he grew close and shook the water from his coat. Instead of coming out in a spray, it appeared as a fine mist.

Sandy tugged at her house coat. "The humidity is horrid. I'm going to need another shower." She looked at Jerry. "Follow me to the house, and I'll get you that key. Wayne and Lori won't be home for a while. They are out playing cards."

Jerry followed as the women used their flashlights to lead the way to the front of the house. Gertie continued to her home across the street, while Sandy cut to the left and went to the house next door.

Sandy stopped before going inside. "If you don't mind waiting here, I'll get the key for you."

As Jerry waited, Gunter nosed around in the woman's flowerbed. The dog's tail curled upwards, and he stretched his head into the greenery. A second later, a large toad hopped out from beneath the plants. Gunter followed after it, flinching each time the toad jumped.

The door clicked, and Sandy returned. “Sorry I had you wait outside, but by now, everyone within view of the house has probably seen you, and I have my reputation to think of.”

Jerry suppressed a chuckle. “Yes, ma’am, I understand.”

Sandy started to hand him the key, then hesitated. “Do you think Wayne and Lori will be upset if I give this to you?”

Jerry added putting Sandy in an awkward position to his list of regrets. While he’d been hoping to surprise his parents, it wasn’t fair to have Sandy betray their trust by giving him the key. He smiled. “You know, I think it would be best if you just give them a call to make sure.”

Sandy blew out a sigh. “Oh, I was hoping you’d say that. I have their number written on the chalkboard next to my telephone. I’ll call Lori right now. You wait right here.”

Jerry held up his cell phone. “We could use my cell instead. I have Mom’s number on speed dial.”

“Of course you do. Too bad you didn’t think to use it earlier. Why, all of this mess could have been avoided.” Sandy smiled. “Bet you won’t make that mistake again.”

“No, ma’am, I reckon I’ve learned my lesson.”

Chapter Five

The moment Jerry opened the door to his parents' house, all the time he'd spent moping about not going home evaporated. While he'd never visited their Florida home before, he'd seen enough of his mother's photos on Facebook that the small house immediately filled in the blanks. His father's recliner sat in the corner of the living room nearest the window. Jerry recognized the small lamp table beside his mother's glider chair, which sat next to the sofa under the front window. The picture frames above the gas fireplace were mostly the same; some had updated photos, but the frames themselves had once sat over a different mantel in a larger room in their Tennessee home.

The kitchen and dining room adjoined the front room. Jerry walked around the small four-seat table and opened the door to the garage. A smile touched his lips as he saw his mother's golf cart – pink from top to bottom, including the loofa hanging from the mirror. While he'd seen photos of what his mother lovingly referred to as the Pink Princess, this was his first time seeing the cart in person. That his mother drove at all still amazed him, as she'd lived most of her adult life without ever having been behind the wheel of a moving vehicle.

Jerry closed the door and walked to the back of the house. Gunter followed, his nails clicking softly on the tile as he lowered his nose and went to work inspecting the space. On the right was his parents' room, a nice-size space that held a king-size bedroom suite and had a private bath with a tiled shower. Jerry closed the door and opened the one on the opposite side of the hall. He switched on the light to find an equally-sized guest bedroom with an en-suite bathroom with a small garden tub.

As he looked about the room, he smiled. Granny's old wooden rocker sat on the opposite side of the room, just as it had in her Tennessee home. Draped across the back of the chair was the multicolored afghan his grandmother had used to cover him whenever he fell asleep.

Gunter lifted his nose, walked to the rocker, and rubbed his face against the crocheted blanket as if he knew its special meaning. Jerry inspected the cluster of frames on the wall to the right of the door, each with pictures of him and his brother Joseph. One of the photos was of them together, each with silly grins plastered on their face. Jerry recognized it as the last photo they'd had taken together the day before he had left for the Marines. His brother had made him promise not to get dead. Jerry had agreed. He often wished he'd made Joseph make the same promise. Jerry swallowed. He turned away, shook off the moment of sorrow, and continued looking about the room. Though the bedroom furniture was new, the room still felt welcoming.

Jerry walked to the back of the room and opened the door to the screened-in porch that stretched around the whole back of the house. He stepped into the moonlit room, which held white rattan furniture with frog print cushions, and pulled the door closed behind him. He heard a noise and turned to watch Gunter push through the closed door.

Jerry shrugged his apologies to the dog. "Sorry, boy."

Gunter ignored him in favor of sniffing a small lizard suctioned to the outer wall. Jerry stood in the dark, listening to the frogs in the swamp. The difference in their sounds attested to the multitude of varieties that made their home within the swamp. Night birds – most of which he'd never heard before – called to each other from within their sanctuary. His heart swelled as a hoot owl called to him from somewhere close by, instantly reminding him of the owl from his childhood. He could see why his mother had fallen in love with this house. Jerry listened for a few more moments before turning and heading back inside. This time, Gunter followed through the open door.

As Jerry entered, he ran his fingers along his grandmother's rocker listening to the wood rock against the cool tile. From the recesses of his mind, he heard Granny's voice gently scold him for unsettling the empty chair. *Don't rock an empty chair, Jerry. Not unless you're ready for company, as you're inviting spirits to come and sit a spell.*

He stilled the chair and smiled. No, this wasn't the home from his childhood, but it had enough memories to make it feel like home, and for that, he gave thanks.

Jerry returned to the living room and sat on the sofa. He started to reach for the remote and decided against it, opting for his phone. He pulled up TikTok and searched The Villages. He clicked on one of the offerings, which claimed The Villages had the highest STD rating in the country. His mouth went dry. Thankfully, the video that followed was from a doctor dispelling the myth. Jerry saw a video showing a loofa chart that claimed each colored loofa represented a sexual preference. Jerry recalled the pink loofa that hung in his mother's golf cart and emitted a whole-body shudder. He closed out the app, fearing further enlightenment.

Gunter barked and jumped from the couch. A

moment later, Jerry heard the garage door rising. He pushed himself up from the couch and went to greet his parents. He stopped at the island, which separated the living space from the kitchen area, and waited.

His mother was the first through the door, her face lighting up when she saw him. She set her purse on the table and wagged her index finger at him. "Jerry Carter McNeal, I don't know whether to yell at you or hug you."

"I'll settle for a hug." He stiffened when she hurried across the room and wrapped her arms around him.

She let go, frowning as she looked him up and down. "What's wrong? Are you hurt? What happened? Were you in a car wreck? Is that why you're driving that tiny car instead of your Durango? Wayne, get in here! Jerry's hurt!"

Jerry patted the air with his hands, hoping to calm her. "Mom, I'm okay, I promise. It's just a couple of cracked ribs. They're on the mend and nothing to worry about."

The color drained from her face. "Fractured ribs? Wayne!"

"What's all the commotion?" his father asked, coming in from the garage carrying several white plastic grocery bags. While his mother had always worked to keep up her appearance, his father sometimes looked haggard, as if years of worry had drained him of his youth. Something had changed since the last time Jerry had seen him; somehow, he looked as if he were now aging in reverse. Wayne sat the bag on the kitchen counter below the island and took in the worried look on Lori's face. "What'd I miss?"

"It's Jerry. His ribs are broken." She worried at her wedding ring, her lips trembling as she turned her attention back to Jerry. "You made it all through the Marines without so much as a scratch, and now you get broken ribs."

"They're cracked, not broken." Jerry looked at his dad, silently pleading with him to intervene. "It's just a couple of cracked ribs. Dad, tell her I'm okay."

Wayne looked him up and down as he started pulling the groceries from the bags. "Jerry says he's okay. Calm down, sweetheart. Jerry is a grown man and should know how he feels."

Lori stood wringing her hands for a moment. "I'm going to go put fresh sheets on the guest bed. You are staying the night here, aren't you, Jerry?"

Jerry smiled. "I'd like to stay for a few days if that's okay."

Lori beamed her delight. "Of course, it's okay. Why, you can stay for a month if you'd like." Lori left without waiting for him to reply. Gunter followed after her, his tail wagging.

Jerry eyed his dad. "A month?"

Wayne chuckled. "Your mother's referring to

The Villages bylaws. We can have guests for up to a month without anyone raising an eye."

Jerry glanced at the bags and saw his favorite cereal and a box of toaster pastries. "I thought you two were playing cards."

Wayne jerked a thumb in Lori's direction. "We were until we found out you were here. Your mother insisted we stop by the store to pick up a few things before we came home. She hurried up and down each aisle, saying Jerry likes this, and Jerry likes that while tossing things into the cart."

Jerry sighed. "That's why I didn't tell you I was coming. I knew Mom would spend the whole time in the kitchen making all my favorite food."

"You should have called. You know she would have loved cooking for you. Besides, I miss your mother's cooking." Wayne shut the cabinet and lowered his voice. "Lori rarely cooks anymore. She likes to go to restaurants in the square."

"Doesn't that get redundant?" Jerry asked, keeping his voice low.

"We have many to choose from, which keeps things interesting." Wayne grabbed the milk from the bag and slid it into the fridge. "But if you mean eating out in general, you tell me. You're the one living on the road."

"It does." Jerry recalled the breakfast April had made for him while in Virginia and smiled. "Every now and then, I luck into a home-cooked meal."

Wayne raised an eyebrow. "From the look on your face, it must have been some meal."

Jerry hid the smile – he wasn't ready to get into that at the moment. "I had a run-in with one of your neighbors."

"Sandy, I know. She called from your phone, remember? You didn't hurt your head in the wreck, did you?"

"I didn't get hurt in the wreck. My Durango did. The cracked ribs are from a climbing accident." Jerry held up a hand. "Long story. I'll fill you both in later. Right now, I want to know how Sandy and Gertie – who pulled a gun on me by the way – seem to know a lot about me."

Wayne chuckled. "Sandy told me about the gun. She said Gertie caught you trying to break into the place."

"I was checking for a key. I don't know what you find so funny. The woman could have shot me."

"Only if you gave her reason. Gertie's husband was a detective – she knows how to shoot. Heck, she should. They went out shooting twice a week right up until the week he died. Heart attack; didn't see it coming. The doctor called it a widow-maker. Gertie took over watching the street after his death. She's astute for her age. I assure you nothing gets past that woman. It's like having our own private security guard in the neighborhood."

Gunter came back into the room and began

nosing around the kitchen.

Jerry scratched his head. "Was her husband's name Herbert?"

"It sure was." Wayne looked about the room. "He's not here, is he?"

Jerry shook his head. "No, but she seemed to be talking to him earlier."

Wayne slid a glance in his direction. "Seemed to be?"

Jerry rubbed at the back of his neck. "She was talking to someone or at least thought she was. I never did see him. Of course, it was dark out. The moon kept slipping in and out of the clouds, so that may have been the reason." While he hadn't felt a presence, Jerry knew from experience that spirits could manifest to a single person without anyone else seeing them. Both Granny and his brother Joseph had appeared to Savannah without his knowledge, even though he was sitting across from her. Though it was rare for Jerry not to see the apparition, it wasn't unheard of. Jerry circled to his earlier question. "Speaking of spirits, the ladies seemed to know a lot about me and knew about Gunter. Any idea where they got their information?"

Before his father could answer, Lori returned to the room. "It's late. You two can talk in the morning. I ran you an Epsom salt bath. I want you to get in there while it's hot and stay until it cools off."

Jerry looked at his father. "Did I just get sent to

my room?"

Wayne gave a half-shrug. "Sounds like she's putting us both to bed. You'd better go on and do as she says. I'll grab your things from the car and place them in your room."

Jerry didn't like asking for help and started to object but knew he would have ended up asking the man to bring them in eventually. He smiled and handed his father his keys. "Thanks, Pop."

Wayne started to leave and hesitated. "I'm sorry if I spoke out of turn telling people about you. I just…"

"I know," Jerry replied, cutting him off.

"The dog, he's here?"

Jerry smiled. "Getting ready to follow you out the door."

Wayne turned to leave. Jerry watched as his father held the door open a bit longer than he would have at any other time.

Chapter Six

Jerry woke feeling more relaxed than he had felt in longer than he could remember. He rolled to his side and was met by a K-9 smile from Gunter, who was sleeping next to him on the queen bed and hogging half of Jerry's pillow. Before Jerry could stop him, Gunter snaked out his tongue and gave Jerry a good morning kiss.

Jerry wiped his face and ruffled the dog's fur. "No offense, dog, but I'd prefer to be waking up to someone with a lot less hair covering their body. Not to mention the fact that you have dog breath."

Gunter growled.

Jerry smiled. "Don't get all bent out of shape. I hadn't dreamed I'd be sleeping in my parents' guest room alone at my age either, so who am I to complain."

Gunter's lip curled into the smile of a dog who

looked at him as if to say, *But here you are, living your best life.*

Jerry rolled to the opposite side of the bed and sat, taking inventory of his body. While he was not healed, he had to admit to feeling less sore than when he'd arrived. He put on his rib brace and went to the dresser to pick out his clothes, mentally patting himself on the back for deciding to unpack his bags the night before. Though he hadn't planned on staying more than a few days, the thought of relaxing in one place for more than a couple of nights had its merits. He could use a vacation. What better place than here, with nothing to do but rest and unwind? He glanced over his shoulder at Gunter. "I'd like to stay for a bit. What do you think?"

Gunter beat the bed with his tail.

"I didn't think you'd mind. Just wait until I tell Dad you like ice cream. You'll have all you can eat. I can assure you of that. Dad is a long-time ice cream connoisseur."

Gunter turned onto his back and then rolled from side to side as if scratching an itch. When he stopped, he remained on his back with his legs in the air and head to the side, staring at Jerry with a wide-open grin.

Jerry matched his grin. "Glad to see you approve. Now off the bed so I can make it. Staying in my parents' house is one thing. Expecting Mom to wait on me hand and foot is another. I'm going to put my foot down and tell her I'm not a little boy anymore and don't need to be treated like one."

The words had no sooner come out of his mouth than there was a knock upon the door. "Jerry, are you awake?"

"Yes, Mom."

"Okay, I made your favorite cinnamon rolls. They will be coming out of the oven in ten minutes. I know how you like them hot with the icing dripping over them," Lori called through the door.

Oh, man, so much for not being treated like a child. While the thought of his mother's homemade cinnamon rolls caused his mouth to water, it also meant his mother had been up for hours, baking from scratch, just to try to please him. Jerry swallowed his guilt. "I'll be right out, Mom."

The smell of his childhood hit him the moment he opened the door. Lori was closing the oven door when he reached the snack bar. Jerry inhaled. "That smells incredible."

Gunter walked to the kitchen area, sniffing the air as Lori sectioned a hot cinnamon roll onto the plate and handed it to him. Jerry took a bite and closed his eyes, savoring the delicacy. "This is incredible." He rounded the counter and poured himself a cup of coffee. He held out the pot. "Want a cup?"

"Sure, my cup is the pink one, but you probably already knew that."

Jerry poured her a cup and handed it to her. "I'm sure I would have eventually gotten it right. Where's Dad?"

"Golfing. He wasn't sure what time you'd get up, and he already had it planned, so he went. He shouldn't be too much longer. You want to sit at the bar or the table?"

"Table's fine. Do you have a special spot?"

Lori shook her head. "No, we rarely eat at home anymore."

"Dad said you enjoy eating out."

Lori sat her cup and plate on the table and stared at him wide-eyed. "Wayne said that?"

Uh oh. Jerry nodded.

"Well, if that don't beat all. Whenever I mention cooking, your father tells me not to bother. He says that's why we moved here, so that we can have the full Villages experience. I have to go to the gym six days a week and swim every day to keep my weight under control."

"If it makes you feel any better, you look great. Dad too. I can't remember ever seeing him looking this good."

Lori took a drink of coffee and smiled. "That's because of you."

Jerry eyed her over his cup. "Me?"

"Because of your talk at Marvin's. I'm telling you, your father's a changed man. Full of life and just plain happy. He used to be an introvert but not anymore. He has friends. The man has never had friends. Now he's always going golfing or doing other things guys do."

"Does it bother you?" Jerry asked.

The lines in her brow creased. "Why on earth would it bother me?"

"I just want to make sure he still has time for you."

She smiled. "I assure you, your father is just as attentive as always. He's a good man, Jerry. He always has been." Lori's smile disappeared. "If it weren't for your father, I don't know how I would have survived Joseph's death."

"I'm sorry, Mom, I didn't mean to…"

"Don't you apologize for making me remember my son!" She softened her tone. "I didn't mean to yell. That isn't what this conversation is about. It is about the change that's come over your father since the two of you made peace. He is so proud of you. Why, he tells everyone about you."

Jerry recalled his conversation with Sandy and Gertie. "Yeah, I know."

Lori raised an eyebrow. "What's that supposed to mean?"

"Dad told them about my gift, and they know about Gunter."

"And?"

Jerry lowered his fork. "What do you mean and?"

"Just what I said. What is wrong with a man bragging about his son?"

"Mom, it's one thing to say, 'I'm proud of my son; he's a cop.' And another to say, 'My son talks to ghosts and has a ghost dog who travels with him.'"

"Are you ashamed of what you do?"

"No."

"You answered that pretty quickly."

"That's because I've accepted my gift."

"It's about time. What about the dog? Are you ashamed of him?"

"Ashamed of Gunter? No, why should I be?"

Lori smiled. "You shouldn't be. But something has you out of sorts. Your father hasn't said anything that wasn't true, so why should it bother you who he tells?"

When put like that, he didn't have a reasonable comeback. "I don't know. I guess I've just kept it to myself. You know how the kids were in school."

"You're not in school anymore, Jerry. You're an adult with an extraordinary gift. One you should be proud of. One your father is proud of. There are plenty of men in The Villages that can say their son is a police officer. But your father is the only one I know who can say his son is the Lead Paranormal Investigator with the FBI."

"I don't work for the FBI, Mom. I work for…" Jerry stopped. How could he tell her when even he didn't know?

"I know, it's some secret agency that you're not allowed to talk about. That's why your father tells people it's the FBI – he doesn't want to get you in trouble." Lori reached a hand across the table and laid it across his. "Don't take this away from him."

Jerry sighed. If his father wanted to brag about him to a couple of his neighbors, what harm could it do? "Okay, Mom."

"I'll be right back. I have to visit the ladies' room." Lori pushed back from the table and hurried from the room.

Jerry looked at Gunter. "I guess we'd better get used to being celebrities while we're here. Wait? Is that drool? Are you okay?" Jerry remembered the frog and wondered if maybe Gunter had eaten it and gotten sick. *Don't be ridiculous, McNeal. Dead dogs can't get sick. Perhaps not, but something was wrong. Why else would the dog be drooling?* Jerry picked up his phone and typed the phrase *why is my dog drooling* and skimmed through the answers, one of which stated it could be watching Jerry eat. Jerry set his phone down. "You've seen me eat before. Why should this bother you now?"

Gunter woofed.

Jerry scraped his fork against the plate, and Gunter licked his lips. Jerry looked at his plate. "What, the cinnamon roll?"

Gunter barked an excited bark.

Jerry went to the counter, grabbed another roll, and returned to his seat. He cut a small piece and offered it to Gunter. To his surprise, the dog took it from him, scarfing it down without chewing. "You have a sweet tooth! It's not just ice cream. You like sugar!"

Gunter licked his lips once more.

Jerry gave him another bite and another until, at last, the roll was gone. He thought about placing his plate on the floor to let Gunter lick it clean but was afraid his mother would throw the whole thing away.

Lori came back into the room. She stopped at Jerry's chair, placed her hands on Jerry's shoulders, and leaned down, putting her cheek against his. "I'm so glad you're here, Jerry. It's nice to have you home again."

Jerry smiled. "It's good to be home, Mom." As the words came out of his mouth, he knew they were not just words. They were the truth.

Lori looked at the clock and frowned.

"Problem?"

"No, not really. I was supposed to get my hair done today, but I don't want to leave you here by yourself."

Jerry laughed. "I'm thirty-two years old, Mom. I don't need a babysitter."

"I know, but you just got here."

"And I will be staying a few days." He knew better than to commit to any more. Stretching his visit would be acceptable; leaving early would seem as though he were running away. "Please go to your appointment and any other activities that you have scheduled during my visit. I came here to relax, not interrupt your and Dad's schedule."

Lori smiled. "If I leave now, I can just make it."

Lori started gathering the dishes from the table, and Jerry stood. "I'll take care of the dishes. Go."

She smiled and hurried to her bedroom, returning a moment later with her purse and keys. "Don't bother with the dishes; just place them in the sink. I'll get them when I get back."

Jerry took her by the shoulders and turned her toward the door. "Go." He followed her to the garage, pushed the button to raise the door, and watched as she climbed into the pink cart and sped away as if she'd been driving it all her life. He was still marveling at her progress as he lowered the garage door. As he turned, he saw a sight he never thought he'd see. Gunter stood with his feet on the table, chasing the plate with his tongue. Jerry signaled him down. Gunter took one last lick before lowering to the floor. Jerry wagged his finger at the dog. "That is not okay."

Gunter licked his lips.

Jerry hardened his voice. "Did you hear me? I said that was not okay. If my mother had seen you, she would kick us both out."

Gunter looked to the counter and licked his lips.

"No, you can't have another one. Not after that little stunt."

Gunter planted his feet and snorted.

"No means no."

Gunter lowered to the floor and placed his head on his paws.

"That's more like it."

Jerry claimed the dishes from the table, placed them in the sink, and then rooted through the cabinets until he found a container suitable for keeping the cinnamon rolls fresh. He dug them out one by one, placing them in the container. When he was finished, he started to add the pan to the sink. Thinking better of it, he placed it on the floor in front of Gunter. "You have until I finish washing the others before I take it."

Gunter lifted his eyes and looked at him as if to say, *Boy, I've got you trained.*

Chapter Seven

The morning air lacked the humidity of the evening prior. Jerry took a cup of coffee to the screened porch and sat looking out over the swamp. Though he could still hear the frogs, the night birds had been replaced with the familiar sounds of birds that preferred the light of day. Gunter seemed content to stay within the confines of the porch, sitting in a chair, ears twitching as he watched several large white cranes picking their way through the swamp.

Jerry snapped a picture of Gunter sitting in the chair and sent it to Max. He waited for a response, then sighed when he didn't get one. He drummed his fingers on the chair, debating whether to send the photo to April, then decided against it. If Max found it as amusing as he, she would show it to her mom. *Yes, but it would give you a reason to start a conversation with April. And what if she doesn't answer? But suppose she does? Wouldn't it be nice to hear April's voice, even if it was written in a text?* Jerry hovered his finger over the phone for several seconds before finally deciding against it as April's words rang in his ears. *It's not like there's any chemistry between us.* Only there was, at least on his end, and he missed both April and Max more than he'd ever missed anyone else. *I think you're in love, McNeal. Was it true? Was he truly in love or simply tired of being alone?*

Gunter's ears twitched. The dog yipped and disappeared.

Jerry looked toward the swamp, half expecting the dog to materialize, but saw no sign of him. He thought of Max and recalled the time she needed help, and Gunter appeared at her side to save the day. Jerry looked at his phone. *Is that why Max isn't answering, because she's in trouble?* His heart began to race. He pulled up her number and pressed send, pressing the phone to his ear and waiting for her to respond. When she didn't answer, he called April.

"Hello?"

"April? Is everything okay? Is Max with you?"

"Jerry? Max is upstairs. She's fine. What's wrong? Did something happen?"

"Are you sure she's alright? Maybe you should check."

"Hang on."

Jerry listened as April's words became muffled and realized she'd covered the phone to keep from yelling in his ear.

She uncovered the phone. "Max is fine. She and her friend Chloe are upstairs painting each other's nails. Why the sudden concern?"

Jerry breathed a sigh of relief. "Sorry, I didn't mean to bother you. Gunter disappeared, and I got worried."

"Gunter's missing? How long has he been gone?" April asked.

"No, he's not missing. Not really. He just disappeared. He barked before he left, and I thought maybe there was trouble." Jerry realized he probably sounded like a total doofus.

April's voice calmed. "I don't know where he went, but he's not here. I know because the house would be filled with schoolgirl giggles if he were."

She was right, of course, but it had given him a legitimate reason to call. "I'm glad everything's okay. How was your flight?"

"It was perfect from start to finish. I don't know how Fred managed it, but he had my car waiting at the airport when we got back to Michigan. Seriously, the man is the can-do man. If you need it done, that man can do it."

Jerry laughed. "I agree. Sometimes I think old Fred has a magic wand, and he waggles it when we're not looking. That's the only thing that would explain it."

"You might be right. I'll keep a closer watch next time we are near him. Did you make it to your parents' house?"

"I did. I'm sitting on the screened-in porch looking at the swamp."

"Swamp. You mean with alligators?"

"I haven't seen any, but it's Florida. I'm sure they are in there."

"If you do see any, send Max a picture. I'm sure she'll get a kick out of seeing it and showing it to her friends."

"Okay, will do." Jerry searched for something else to say to keep her on the phone. "Any big plans for the holidays?"

"No, nothing too big. Max and I are going to my friend Carrie's for dinner. How about you?"

"I'm going to hang out here for a bit. I was dreading coming down, but it's not as weird as I thought it would be."

"They're your parents. Why would it be weird?"

"This is going to sound corny, but I wasn't sure it would feel like home since it isn't where I grew up."

"I thought you said you spent more time at your grandmother's house."

That she remembered their conversation made him smile. "I did, but the holidays were always family time with aunts, uncles, cousins, and whoever else happened to show up."

"It sounds nice."

"Oh, it was awful. No one ever got along, but everyone was together, which made it better."

"I envy people with big families who like to be around each other. I never had that, and neither has Max."

I'd like to change all of that. While Jerry ached to say the words out loud, he kept the thought to himself. He was enjoying talking to April too much to risk rejection. "If it makes you feel better, I've already had a gun pulled on me. That's how much fun I'm having."

"A gun! Why would that make me feel better?"

Jerry chuckled. "It shouldn't. I was just trying to lighten the mood. It happened right after I got here. The old woman across the street thought I was trying to break in."

"Oh, no."

Jerry shook his head. "Yes, it was quite the welcoming party."

"I'm surprised they let them have guns."

Jerry frowned at the phone. "Them?"

"The old people."

Jerry suppressed a laugh. "It's a retirement community, not an old people's home." Jerry recalled the videos he'd watched on his phone, talking about what went on in The Villages. "I assure you most of the people here have a lot of life left in them."

April laughed an easy laugh. "Goes to show what I know. I thought you were kidding about it being the party capital of the world."

He remembered the pink loofa hanging from the mirror of his mother's golf cart. *I wish I were kidding.* "Nope."

"Good. You need to loosen up. You always seem too serious. Maybe you'll get invited to a few parties."

Jerry shuddered. "I hope not."

"Maybe they play charades."

"What?"

"At the parties. I was just wondering what old people do when they go to a party."

"Cards." At least that was what they'd told him. *What if...Don't go there, McNeal. Once you get that picture in your head, there's no getting it out.*

"Nice. If you find out any different, send me some pictures."

Another shudder. "I'm not much of a community card player."

"Sure you are; you just need to step out of your comfort zone, Jerry. I bet your mom and dad would love for you to play cards with their friends. Embrace your family."

Just when Jerry thought he would have to tell her about the things that went on at The Villages, the door clicked open, and Wayne stepped outside carrying two bottles of water and a plate with three cinnamon rolls.

"Hey, my dad's back. I've got to go." While he hated ending the call, he was happy not to be continuing that particular conversation.

"Okay, Jerry. Have fun."

"I'll try." Jerry ended the call and smiled. He was glad he'd called and even happier that the conversation hadn't felt strained. Maybe Granny was right. Perhaps April had pushed him away to keep from getting hurt. If that was the case, then perhaps he still had a chance with her.

Wayne handed him a bottle of water and held out the plate. "Want a roll?"

Jerry shook his head. "No thanks. I've already had three."

Wayne set the plate on the side table and looked out over the swamp. "What do you think of our backyard?"

Jerry looked at the small stretch of grass that was cordoned off from the swamp with what looked to be railroad ties. "There's not much to it."

"I like it that way. Not much to take care of, but I was talking about the swamp."

"The swamp's cool. Get many gators in the yard?"

"I haven't seen any come up here, but I've seen them in the swamp. The best part is, except for a shift in the lily pads, the view will never change."

"It's a nice place, Dad. I can see why you and Mom bought it," Jerry said sincerely.

Wayne turned and leaned against the back wall. "I assume your mother is at the salon?"

"Yep." Until this moment, Jerry had always thought he resembled his mother, but seeing his father standing there in that position, he could clearly see himself. Had the resemblance always been there, and he was just too bullheaded to see it? "I have to tell you it was really something watching her get into that golf cart and scooting away like that."

"I'm surprised she agreed to go with you being here and all."

Jerry opened his water and took a long drink. "I promised to be here when she gets back."

Wayne started to sit and looked at Jerry. "Is the dog in the chair?"

Jerry sighed. "No, he disappeared a few minutes ago."

"Disappeared? You have no idea where he went?"

Jerry smiled. "It's not like he told me where he was going."

Wayne swiped his finger across the plate to gather the icing and plucked it into his mouth. "Wouldn't surprise me if he did."

Jerry took another drink. "Honestly, sometimes I

expect him to talk."

"Are you enjoying your new job?" Wayne asked.

"If you can call it that."

"What do you mean?"

Jerry shrugged a shoulder. "I'm basically doing what I've been doing since leaving Pennsylvania."

Wayne frowned. "Your mom said you caught a serial killer. I don't recall you doing that in Pennsylvania."

"Technically, the dog caught him," Jerry corrected.

"But the dog is attached to you?"

"Yes."

Wayne smiled. "You never were one to accept the things you can do."

Jerry started to tell him it would have been easier to accept his gift if Wayne had been more supportive but decided against it. He was here to relax, not open old wounds. "I did help the FBI with a case they were working on. Me and Max; she's this girl that has the gift."

"Yes, your mom told me about her. She's like you?"

Jerry shook his head. "No, that kid is amazing. I think she's better than me, and as she matures, there will be nothing she can't do."

"You seem to care a lot about her."

Jerry smiled. "Yes, Max and her mother are great."

Wayne raised an eyebrow. "From the looks of that smile, I'd say you're pretty fond of the mother too."

"They're great people."

"Sounds serious."

"I thought there could be something between us. I'm not convinced April feels the same way."

"Maybe she's just playing hard to get. Your mother wouldn't have anything to do with me at first."

"Really? I guess the way you two act, I thought it had been love at first sight."

"It wasn't even love at second sight. At least not on your mother's end – I had to work at it." Wayne picked up a roll and took a bite. "I guess you can say I pestered her until she finally gave in. It was worth it. That woman has given me many happy years. She's happy to have you here. We both are."

"I'm happy to be here. If I start to wear out my welcome, just let me know, and I'll take off."

"What's that supposed to mean?"

"Only that I know you and Mom have your own lives, and I don't want to get in the way of things."

Wayne raised an eyebrow. "Things?"

"I saw the loofa on Mom's cart. I know what goes on in the bubble."

Wayne licked the icing from his fingers. "I guess the cat's out of the bag. Why do you think we had to have a two-bedroom? Why, we've been hosting couples' retreats ever since we moved."

Jerry felt his stomach churn.

His father chuckled. "Give your imagination a rest, son. Your mother and I are not part of any swingers' club."

Jerry so wanted to believe him. "What about the loofa?"

"It's to help your mom find her golf cart. I have one on the car too. Lots of people have them for the exact same reason. You'd think there would only be one pink golf cart, but I assure you that's not the case. Some put their loofas on the roof, and others tie them elsewhere. It's a vehicle finder and nothing more."

"What about the other rumors?"

Wayne leaned forward in his chair. "Son, let me share a word of advice with you – don't believe anything you hear and only half of what you see." As the words of wisdom left his father's mouth, Gunter appeared at his side, stealthily lifting a cinnamon roll from the plate and swallowing it in one bite. Wayne sat back in his seat and looked at his plate. "My memory seems to be going. I don't remember eating two."

Jerry looked to the spot where Gunter now sat, eyeing the last roll. "You didn't."

Wayne's eyes grew wide. "Gunter? I thought you said he doesn't eat."

Jerry shrugged. "It started with ice cream.

Today, he progressed to Mom's cinnamon rolls. It seems the dog has developed a sweet tooth."

Chapter Eight

Jerry sat in the front of the pink golf cart as Lori drove through The Villages giving him a guided tour. Jerry was amazed at how well his mother navigated the vast community until she'd let him in on her secret by showing him the golf cart app on her phone, which allowed her to see where she was going – a good thing, since she'd told him there were over one hundred miles of golf cart paths. As it was, the app helped her navigate bridges and tunnels with ease while cruising past miles and miles of golf courses.

Wayne sat on the back of the cart, delighted with the knowledge that Gunter sat next to him. It didn't matter that his father couldn't see the dog, Jerry had told him Gunter was there, and that was all his dad needed as proof – total blind faith, all because of a missing cinnamon roll.

Lori slowed and pointed to a pond. "Look, Jerry, there's an alligator. I don't know his name."

Jerry pulled his phone free and took a picture for Max. "They name them?"

"Some of them. There was a big one named Larry, but he was a bad boy and took a walkabout to the golf shop in Brownwood. Some people complained, so they relocated him to an alligator farm. There were some babies in the pond the other day. Hopefully, the birds haven't eaten them all."

Jerry looked over the pond. "What kind of bird eats alligators?"

"Blue Heron." Lori let off the gas, and the cart began moving once more. "It bothered me the first time I saw it, but I guess it's part of nature."

"There was a gator on the golf course this morning. John had to wait for him to cross before taking his turn."

Jerry looked over his shoulder. "Aren't you afraid they'll come after you?"

"Nope, John's ten years older than I am. I don't have to outrun the gator. I just have to outrun John and Al – he's the other fellow I golf with. There are over fifty, you know."

Jerry frowned. "Alligators?"

"No, golf courses."

"No, I didn't know that."

"Moving here was the best decision your mom and I ever made. I'm telling you Jer, the place is like

Disneyland for adults. You name it, this place has it: dancing, a movie theater, performing arts, shopping, and pretty much any restaurant you can think of. Golf, tennis, pickleball; again, if you can think of it, then it's probably here. Why, some of our friends don't even own cars."

"You said movie theater. Is there just one?"

Lori sighed. "Yes, there used to be more, but I guess some things are changing. They are turning ours in Spanish Springs into a gym. I use the gym more than I go to the movies, but I know there are some not that happy with it." She laughed. "We old people can be set in our ways. I don't think I would have ever gotten your father to give up his flip phone if he hadn't needed the apps to navigate the golf cart paths or set up his tee times."

Jerry nodded. "I understand, Pops. Nothing I hate worse than changing phones."

Gunter barked. Jerry looked to see a woman walking a silver standard poodle. Jerry wagged a finger at the back seat. "Don't you even think about it."

"Think about what?" Wayne asked. "What did I do?"

Jerry laughed and pointed to the woman walking her dog. "Not you; Gunter. He's a player."

Lori nearly drove off the path. "You mean to tell me he can…"

Jerry cut her off. "Yep."

"How is that even possible?" Wayne asked over the seat.

Jerry shrugged. "You two ought to know – you're the ones who told me about the birds and bees."

"Last I recall, the birds and the bees weren't ghosts," Lori remarked, speeding off. She looked in the mirror and then handed her cell phone to Wayne. "It's time to head back to Spanish Springs. Will you plug in the address?"

Jerry felt his neck tingle. "What's in Spanish Springs?"

"Your father and I want to introduce you to a few of our friends. We're meeting them in the square." Wayne handed Lori her phone, which she placed in the holder. Lori looked in the mirror again, then glanced at Jerry. "Quit looking so glum, son. It's not like we're taking you to one of our swingers' parties."

Jerry felt his heart rate increase.

"Lighten up, Jerry, I'm just messing with you. Your dad told me you'd been watching those TikTok videos." Lori flicked the loofa hanging from the rearview mirror and giggled. "I can't believe you thought your father and I were swingers. And at our age. I assure you the only thing your father swings is a golf club, and to hear him talk, he's not very good at it."

"Hey, I'll have you know I'm getting better. If

they ever make any of those holes par nine instead of par three, I will be on ESPN."

Lori glanced at Jerry. "What your father is saying is he does a lot of swinging, but he's not actually hitting anything."

***

Lori parked the Pink Princess at the curb alongside several others. As they walked toward the pavilion, Jerry felt his mother's energy increase. Maybe that was because more than two dozen people were sitting in green chairs under the structure, each staring in their direction. Lori whispered to Wayne, "I thought you said you only invited a couple of friends."

"I did. I don't know who half of those people are. Maybe it's just a coincidence they are here."

Jerry looked toward the small group and noticed multiple spirits among them. The energy within the group was palpable. Jerry knew every one of them, both living and dead, expected something of him. Gunter must have felt it too, as the dog had not left his side since jumping from the cart. If the energy had been calm, the dog would be inspecting the crowd, not pressing against Jerry's leg as if to give them both comfort.

Wayne took the lead. Jerry slowed his pace, and Lori moved to his other side. "Whatever happens today, I want you to know your father means well."

Jerry stopped. "What do you mean whatever

happens? What is going on, Mom?"

Lori glanced at the crowd and then worried at her wedding ring. "You know your father told his friends about you."

"I do."

"Well, they want to meet you."

"This doesn't look like a meeting. It looks like a trial."

Lori smiled a weak smile. "No, Jerry, it's not like that. It's just, well, you know, people are curious. They want to know things."

"What kind of things?"

"I would only be guessing, but I suppose maybe they want you to tell them about their lives and help them contact their loved ones."

Jerry stiffened. "You mean give them readings?"

Lori nodded her head. "Yes. I suppose that's what they're called."

"Mom, that's not what I do." Jerry felt the panic starting to rise. He glanced at the crowd, and suddenly, he was a young boy standing in the school play yard facing his classmates. The children had learned of his gift and stood staring at him, waiting to see what magic he could produce for them. It was his friend, Randy Smuth, who'd told of Jerry's secrets when Jerry had gotten brave enough to confess to his friend the things he was able to do. Only, it wasn't magic, at least not as they were led to believe. Jerry couldn't turn it on or off, nor could he concentrate with such intense energy being sent his way. They'd bombarded him with questions and taunted him relentlessly when he hadn't been able to answer. It wasn't that Jerry hadn't wanted to answer – he just didn't know how to channel the energy at the time and still had difficulty navigating crowds. That experience had done much to shape his childhood and was a significant reason he'd run from his gift for so many years. He locked eyes with his mother, begging her to understand. "I can't do this, Mom."

"Of course you can. I've seen you do it. Here comes your father. Look how proud he is."

Wayne walked toward them in long, confident strides and grinned a wide grin when he reached them. "I guess my friend John let the cat out of the bag. I told him you were here and that I wanted him and Al to meet you. He asked if he could bring a couple of friends. Near as I can tell, all of them also brought friends. Come on, son, and I'll introduce you."

Jerry dug his heels in. "Dad, I don't do readings and don't do well in crowds, especially where everyone wants something from me."

Lori smiled. "You're just nervous. How about we take a walk over there and say hello? You don't have to do anything that makes you uncomfortable."

I'm already uncomfortable. Tell her, McNeal. Tell her the hairs on the back of your neck are vibrating like tiny cattle prods. He searched his parents' faces and knew to say no would shred the fence they'd mended in recent months. Instead of refusing, he allowed Lori to hook her elbow into his and lead him toward the source of his anxiety.

All the folks sitting in the green plastic chairs stared at him as he approached. Each appeared to be double his age, nicely dressed, and yet the way they looked at him did nothing to ease his anxiety as each face was filled with morbid curiosity.

Death. That was what he felt. Not that the people sitting in front of him were going to die, not at this moment anyway. But that was what each one wanted to know – what happens next. Not in the next few moments, but next in their journey. That was what they came here to find out, and that was the one question Jerry could not answer.

Jerry turned away from the source of his anxiety.

"Jerry?" Lori called after him.

"Let him go, dear," his father said softly. "I shouldn't have made him come."

Jerry stormed to the edge of the pavilion, stopping when Gunter moved in front, blocking his way. Jerry started to step around the dog. Gunter growled. "What do you want from me, dog? You're supposed to be on my side."

A hand touched his shoulder. Jerry knew without looking that Granny was standing beside him. *I'm here too, Jerry,* she told him without speaking. It was a gift they had shared even when she was alive.

While Jerry was glad she was there, he wanted nothing more than to run away. *I can't do this, Granny. Tell the dog to move.*

Do what, Jerry?

Tell them what they want to know. You remember what happened the last time. Those kids. I can still see their faces.

Turn around, Jerry.

Jerry did as he was told.

What do you see? Granny's voice was a calm presence in a sea of uncertainty.

A crowd of people. There are too many. They all want – I don't know what they want because they are all yelling at me – each vying for my attention. It's no use. I can't help them. Not with all that yelling.

Granny moved behind him and placed her hands on his shoulders, instantly calming him. *Don't think of them as a group. Separate them. Look at each as a single person who has come to seek something from you. Something only you can provide. You didn't hesitate to help Patty, Rita, or the others when they came to you for help. This is what you do, Jerry. It is what you were born to do.*

Jerry searched the crowd, considering each face. Not kids ready to laugh and ridicule him, but adults clinging to hope. As he singled out individual faces, his panic ebbed. Suddenly, he could hear each thought in turn. *I can hear them. It's still like they are all talking, but I can hear each thought. What if I can't answer their questions?*

Then tell them that.

They'll be disappointed.

Don't take on that guilt, Jerry. That is not what this is about. Not everyone gets to be a winner – some will get their answers, others are meant to learn on their own. The only thing you need to do is listen and answer when you can.

As if a weight had lifted from his shoulders, Jerry's breath now came easy. He walked to where his father was standing. "I'm sorry, Dad. I'm ready to meet your friends."

"Are you sure? I shouldn't have sprung this on you as I did."

Jerry felt Gunter lean into his leg. He glanced down at the dog, who lifted his head and looked at him as if to say, *You're not alone. You'll never be alone again.* Jerry peered into the crowd, singled out a woman wearing bold red lipstick, and smiled. "It's okay, Pop. I just needed a moment to get my head together."

Chapter Nine

After his father made the introductions, Jerry spoke to those sitting in the chairs. Instead of looking at the crowd as a whole, he focused on one person at a time, talking to them and them alone, telling of what he saw for them. It was the first time he'd given readings – until today, he didn't know he could.

A man with a goatee stood and asked the question Jerry had been dreading. "What happens after we die?"

Jerry steadied himself and gave the only response he had. "I have no idea."

The man huffed. "What do you mean you don't know? Are you the portal to the other side or not?"

Jerry focused on the man. "No, sir, I am not. I sometimes know things before they happen, and I see and speak with spirits, but I am not a portal."

The man wasn't satisfied. "You claim to see and talk to ghosts, yet you're telling me you have never asked what's on the other side?"

"No, sir, that's not what I said. I said I don't know. I've asked plenty of times, but there seems to be some rule that spirits are not supposed to tell us what's on the other side."

"You're saying the white light doesn't exist?"

Jerry held firm. "I never said that."

"So, it does exist?"

"What you believe is your belief. I am not here to tell you whether it is real or imagined. I talk to spirits. The ones I have spoken with do not think it prudent that I know what comes next. I know there are spirits. I know my partner is the ghost of a K-9 police dog. I know what I see and don't find it in good taste to go around making things up just because it is what some want to hear."

"So you are saying people are lying about there being a white light?" Goatee Man pressed.

"I'm saying I haven't seen it," Jerry repeated.

A round woman with curly hair waved to get his attention. When Jerry looked in her direction, she stood and cleared her throat. "My late husband has visited me twice weekly over the past two years."

Jerry smiled, glad for the turn in the conversation. "That's nice."

She shook her head. "No, you don't understand. I want you to speak with him. I need him to know that while I really appreciate his visits, I would like him to use someone else. Someone a bit younger, maybe someone such as yourself." She looked him up and down and sighed.

The woman was right. Jerry didn't understand. "I'm afraid I'm not following you."

"My friend Bernie and I watched the movie *Ghost* together a few years back, and a week later, my late husband Ernie started inhabiting Bernie's body to come back to..." She looked from side to side as a red blush crept up her face. "He comes back to have relations with me. I've tried to tell him I'd rather him come back as someone a bit taller and with a little more stamina. But he keeps taking over Bernie instead. I mean, Bernie is nice and all, but with all the men he could choose from, I just don't know why he picked him."

Several sitting near her snickered. Jerry worked to keep a straight face. "Ma'am?"

She smiled. "Oh, you don't have to call me that. My name's Connie."

"Yes, ma'am. Connie, is Bernie here?"

Connie tilted her head to the bald gentleman sitting beside her, sweating profusely despite the air being cool and currently squirming in his seat.

Gunter took a step forward, letting out a soft growl.

Jerry eyed the man. "Bernie, are you going to tell her, or am I?"

Bernie stood and looked like a rabbit about to bolt.

Connie turned toward him, all modesty forgotten. "Tell me what?!"

Bernie started to walk away. Connie latched hold of his shirt collar and pulled him back. "I said, tell me what?"

Jerry decided it was time to intervene. "Whose idea was it to watch the movie?"

Connie's face drained of color. "His."

Jerry nodded. "I'm afraid Bernie there has managed to pull a fast one on you. Despite what you see in the movies, spirits don't take over people's bodies in that way. Bernie saw an opportunity and took it. Isn't that right, Bernie?"

When Bernie failed to answer, Connie hit him over the head with her purse and hurried from the pavilion. Bernie sat and rubbed his head. Jerry watched as a woman sitting in the back made her way forward. She walked straight to where Bernie sat and kicked him in the groin with the toe of her shoe. Pulling herself taller, the woman turned and left without a word.

Jerry glanced at his dad. The man arched an eyebrow as the knowledge of what had just transpired passed between them. No words were spoken, not telepathically as with his grandmother, just in the way that let the other know what they were thinking – that Jerry had just put a kibosh to

Bernie's rather ingenious charade.

A spirit stood off to the side. Jerry made eye contact with him, and the apparition disappeared. A moment later, Bernie rose and left without a word.

The woman with the bright red lipstick raised her hand. "I want to see the dog." The others nodded their agreement.

Jerry shook his head. "He doesn't like to show himself."

"That's because he doesn't exist." All eyes turned toward Gertie, who was sitting in the fifth row. "He couldn't see my Herbert either. Mighty convenient if you ask me."

"Is Herbert with you now?" a man sitting in front of her asked.

She looked at Jerry and nodded her head. "He is."

The man turned toward Jerry. "Tell her what he looks like."

Jerry searched the crowd and shook his head. "No can do."

The man frowned. "Why not?"

"Because I can't see him."

Gertie smiled. "But you can see your dog?"

"Yes, ma'am."

"I think you're holding out. I'll give you five hundred dollars cash right now if you admit you can see my husband."

"No, ma'am."

"Why not?"

"Because if I told you I could, then I'd be lying."

Another smile. For a woman not getting what she wanted, Gertie sure seemed happy about it.

"Maybe he's lying about the dog too," someone suggested.

Wayne stepped up beside him. "My son is not a liar. There is a dog."

"You've seen him?" Jerry recognized the voice as belonging to the man with the goatee.

Wayne shook his head. "No, but I've seen him eat a cinnamon roll. Took it right off my plate."

"You just don't remember eating it," the same fellow said.

"My memory is just fine," Wayne told him. "The dog likes sweets."

Lori stepped forward. "Thank you all for coming, but I think it is time for us to leave."

"It's okay, Mom," Jerry assured her.

"No, it is not okay. You didn't want to do this, and now I see why." Lori turned and marched out of the pavilion.

Jerry rolled his neck. "I guess it's time to go."

Wayne nodded his agreement and followed after her. "You might want to let your mother calm down a bit before saying anything."

Jerry ran a hand over the back of his head. "Wait. What did I do?"

"Nothing. But that's not the point. Lori's angry

at herself for pushing you into this. She'll bite your head off without even realizing she's doing it. Trust me on this, and wait until she calms down. She'll talk when she's ready."

Jerry smiled. "You know her pretty well."

Wayne turned and gave a wink. "I should; the woman's had my heart for as long as I've known her."

Jerry sat on the back of the golf cart with Gunter, and Wayne took the seat next to Lori. Not one word was spoken until Lori pulled into the garage, turned off the motor, and headed toward the door that led into the house. As she reached for the doorknob, she hesitated. "Jerry, I don't mind that dog being in the house, but I'll not have his ghost saliva all over my good dishes." Lori went inside without another word.

His mother hadn't raised her voice when saying it – nor had her voice broken when she spoke. It was the most irrational statement made by the most rational woman he'd ever known – and as ludicrous as anything he had heard over the course of the day. As such, it was enough to break the tension that surrounded them.

Wayne scratched his head. "Do ghosts have germs?"

Jerry laughed. "I haven't a clue."

***

Wayne sat in his recliner reading The Villages

newspaper while Lori appeared to be engrossed in a book. Jerry was stretched out on the sofa with Gunter lying next to him, mulling over the events of the day. It didn't matter that things didn't go as well as everyone had hoped. Jerry considered it to be a major breakthrough in something that had plagued him most of his life. While he had hoped visiting his parents would allow for some healing, he didn't realize it would be emotional healing as well as physical.

Jerry scratched Gunter behind the ear, and the dog rolled onto his back so Jerry could rub his belly. Jerry happily obliged.

There was a knock on the door. Lori looked at Wayne. "I'm not expecting anyone. Are you?"

"Nope." Wayne lowered the recliner and walked to the front door. "It's Gertie."

"Tell her to go away." Lori looked at Jerry and shrugged. "I'm still mad at her."

"That wouldn't be very neighborly," Wayne replied, opening the door.

"I brought a peace offering." Gertie handed Wayne a plate of cookies, taking one from the top just before he stepped aside.

Jerry started to get up to make room on the couch. Gertie waved him off, pulling over a kitchen chair instead. She sat, crossed her legs, and held the cookie at her knee. Gunter lifted his head, and Jerry knew the woman had planned her approach. *She's trying to entice him into showing himself. The woman's smooth.* Jerry studied Gertie with a whole new respect. Instantly, he also knew something else. "You lied."

Four sets of eyes turned in his direction. Wayne settled into his recliner. "What'd she lie about, son?"

"When she said her husband was there, I thought maybe I couldn't see him because he didn't want me to, but the real reason I couldn't see him was because he wasn't there."

Instead of being upset at him discovering her ruse, Gertie smiled. "You're very astute, Mr. McNeal."

"It's Jerry. Care to tell me why you lied?"

Lori glared at the woman. "Yes, Gertie, tell us why you were trying to embarrass our son and now have the audacity to come into our house as if we are still friends."

Jerry shook his head. "She wasn't trying to embarrass me. It was a test."

Gertie smiled. "As I said, you are very astute."

"What kind of test?" Lori asked.

"To make sure I wasn't a fraud," Jerry replied.

Wayne looked from Jerry to Gertie. "Did he pass?"

"He did. Had he been a fraud, Jerry would have just agreed with me and been done with it. He wouldn't have had to give me anything personal – he could have blamed it on the distraction of the crowd or any of the numerous things posers do to convince people." Gertie uncrossed her legs and pointed the cookie as she spoke. "I'm still on the fence about the dog, though. That one's gonna take some convincing."

Which is why she's holding the cookie she has yet to take a bite of. Gunter sniffed the air, and Jerry firmed his grip on the dog. Jerry looked at Gertie. "So all that talk when I first arrived of you supposedly speaking to your husband, was that a sham too?"

"No, I hear him. Just probably not in the way you do. When I hear him, it's just his voice in my mind. I don't actually see him. God knows I wish I could, but I haven't."

"The voice you hear could very well be him. Not all spirits appear to us in physical form. I've often heard my grandmother even without her appearing." Jerry made eye contact with his mother. Lori smiled.

"I'm not sure if your parents told you, but my Herbert was a detective. One of his childhood friends had a daughter pass away as a young child. A psychic reached out to her shortly after the child's death and told her he was in contact with the child and could let her talk to her but said it would weaken him mentally and physically, so he would need to be well compensated to consider putting his body through that. The woman, being as distraught as she was, ended up draining her and her husband's savings. Herbert was able to out the man, but it was too late. Between money and the child's death, it ruined her marriage, and the woman never really came out of the depression it caused. After that, Herbert made it his life's mission to oust fakes. I took up the crusade after his passing. Speaking of which, why didn't you arrest Bernie?"

Jerry shrugged. "I'm not sure the case would hold up in court. The guy's a cad, but other than lying, he didn't break any law. It's not like he made the women have sex with him. He told them what they wanted to hear and, except for not being exactly what they wanted looks-wise, seems to have given them something that kept them going back for more."

Gunter sat up and eased off the couch, lowering himself to the floor. Jerry started to recall the dog but decided against it. If the woman wanted convincing, she would soon get her wish.

Chapter Ten

The Villages boasted of having over a hundred and thirty thousand people living within their community. Jerry was beginning to think that every one of them knew about him and Gunter. Not an hour had passed without someone stopping by to drop off pies, cookies, and cake while managing to somehow drop a sweet morsel. Gunter had quickly caught on to the game, lapping up the sugary tidbit, much to the visitor's delight.

The doorbell rang, and Gunter beat a path to the door.

"Whose turn is it to answer?" Wayne called from the comfort of his chair.

"I'll get it." Jerry pushed from the couch and walked the short distance to the door. He opened it to see the man with the goatee standing there holding a tub of ice cream.

The man shrugged his apologies. "I don't bake, and I didn't want to insult the dog by bringing something store-bought."

Jerry eyed the carton and chuckled. "As opposed to buying ice cream out of the freezer case?"

The man frowned at the carton as if trying to figure out the joke. "He doesn't like ice cream? I must have misunderstood. It's strawberry. I was going to get chocolate, but I've read dogs aren't supposed to eat chocolate. Though if he's already dead, I guess it doesn't make a difference."

"Gunter likes ice cream." Jerry backed out of the way to allow the man entrance, then moved to the counter and removed a saucer left there by a previous visitor. He dished out a scoop and placed it on the ground in front of Gunter, who stood drooling even though he'd been eating steadily most of the day.

The man leaned forward, watching the ice cream disappear as Gunter went to work on the cold delicacy. "So that's it? I'm not going to get to see him?"

Jerry shook his head. "Nope. That's the whole of it."

The man bent a little more. "How do I know it's not just melting?"

Jerry cocked an eyebrow. "Because if it were melting, it would still be on the plate."

The guy bobbed his head. "Yes, I suppose you're

right. Splendid, I've never seen a ghost before. I guess technically I still haven't, but it's thrilling all the same."

Jerry expected the man to leave after having his curiosity satisfied. Instead, he walked to the living room. He started for the couch, then reconsidered and sat in the kitchen chair that had been used by many before him. Jerry followed him into the room, shrugging his apologies to his parents, who gawked at the visitor.

The man intertwined his fingers and placed them on his stomach. "So, where do we begin?"

Jerry took his place on the couch. Having finished lapping up his treat, Gunter jumped up beside him, started to sit, and then jumped down again. Walking to where the man sat, the dog went to work sniffing his lower extremities. Jerry wondered if the dog knew something he did not. "How about we start with your name?"

The guy laughed a nervous giggle. "Yes, I suppose that would help. I guess I rather expected you to know it."

Jerry stared at him without blinking. "I'm a psychic, not a mind reader."

"Yes, mind reading is more Uncle Marvin's department," Lori mused.

Jerry ran his hand over his head. While true, he thought it best to let that sleeping dog lie. He caught the man's attention. "Your name?"

"Thomas Snyder. My friends call me Tom."

Jerry smiled. "So, Mr. Snyder, what can I do for you?"

Snyder studied his hands for a moment, then blew out a sigh. "I need to know if I'm going to die."

Jerry worked to keep his face unreadable while wondering if Gunter had truly picked up on something or was simply being his usual rude self. Jerry decided to try the diplomatic approach. "We're all going to die, Mr. Snyder; it's just a matter of when."

Snyder narrowed his eyes. "I'm a well-educated man, Mr. McNeal. As such, I would prefer you not to placate me. I asked a serious question and expect an honest answer. I wish to know if I am to die any time soon."

"Fair enough." Jerry leaned back against the couch, studying the man. While Gunter still seemed interested, Jerry did not feel anything that caused him concern. He shook his head. "No, Mr. Snyder, I do not believe you will."

Snyder let out an audible sigh. "Oh, thank heavens. I have been beside myself ever since my son planned this trip."

Jerry glanced at his parents and then back at Snyder. "Trip?"

"Yes, on an airplane. The boy knows my fear of flying and still insists he is much too busy to pick me up and take me to his house for the holidays this year. I started to object, as my Tiffy doesn't like being left alone, but Mrs. Johnson – she's such a dear – said she would come over and look in on her daily. Anyhow, you leave me with no more excuses. A pity, really. I thought maybe if you saw me dying that I could tell my son of it, and he would have no choice but to come to get me." Gunter moved in for a more thorough sniff, and Snyder squirmed in his seat.

Jerry nodded to the man. "Tiffy wouldn't happen to like sitting in your lap, would she?"

Snyder looked at his pants. "Why yes. She always lies in my lap. Do I have cat hair on me? I thought I had rolled it all off."

A cat. That certainly explained Gunter's infatuation with the man. "No cat hair – at least none that I can see. It's the dog. He seems to be overly interested in your crotch."

"Oh, thank heavens," the man called out for the second time. "I have a new lady friend and thought she might have given me the itch."

Wayne snorted and covered the noise with a cough. While his mother made no comment, she raised the book she'd been reading to hide her face.

"Is there anything else I can do for you, Mr. Snyder?" Jerry asked.

"No, sir. I suppose that will be the whole of it." Snyder rose, started for the door, and hesitated. "It's a shame things couldn't have gone differently over to the square. Some people's kids, you know."

"Yes, sir, I do know," Jerry said, following him to the door. He waited for the man to step out before shutting and locking it behind him.

As soon as Jerry turned, his mother burst out laughing. When she finally got hold of herself, she wiped her eyes with her knuckles. "Jerry, I want to tell you how proud I am of you. I don't know how on earth you can sit there and listen to everything you do without flinching. I thought I was going to burst from holding that in."

"I've had years of practice," Jerry informed her. "Did you catch what he said at the end?"

She stifled another giggle. "Which part?"

"Some people's kids. Granny used to say that anytime she had a problem with someone. Instead of saying their name, she would say 'some people's kids,' as if it was all the parents' fault." Before his mother could answer, the doorbell rang. Jerry sighed. "Remind me to buy a 'do not disturb' sign."

"I could answer and tell them you're not here." Lori offered.

Gunter was standing beside the front door, wagging his tail. Jerry shook his head. "Nah, they'll just come back. Besides, the dog seems to be enjoying his celebrity status."

Jerry opened the door to find no one there. He searched the area before closing it once more. He turned to tell his parents no one was there when

Gunter growled a warning. Jerry saw the spirit standing in the middle of the room and held up a hand to silence his folks. He motioned the man to the chair and returned to his place on the couch. The man was just over six feet tall, neatly dressed in a tailored suit, and his shoes were highly polished. Jerry recognized him as the spirit from the pavilion who disappeared when realizing Jerry had seen him.

"What's wrong?" His mother's words came out in a whisper.

"We have a visitor. Stay calm. There's nothing to worry about." At least he hoped not. The fact that Gunter had positioned himself between their new arrival and his family told him the spirit might not be as friendly as he'd hoped. "What can I do for you, sir?"

"I'm looking for my wife. I want you to help me find her."

"Does your wife live in The Villages?"

"Her name is Bernita Glasco."

Jerry turned toward his dad. "Do you know a Bernita Glasco?"

Wayne shook his head. "I don't. Do you, dear?"

Lori frowned. "No, I've never heard of her."

"Mr. Glasco thinks she lives here."

"Dr."

Jerry looked at the spirit. "Excuse me?"

"I'm Dr. Mortimer Glasco, not Mr."

"The guy was a doctor."

The spirit cleared his throat. "Does that mean you were a Marine?"

Jerry smiled. "Is."

"What, son?" Lori asked.

"I mistakenly said the man *was* a doctor. He informed me he *is* a doctor. Just like I will always be a Marine."

Dr. Glasco smiled. "Now, about finding my wife."

Jerry drummed his fingers on the couch. That the spirit wasn't able to find her himself was somewhat troubling. "I will do some digging and see what I can do."

Dr. Glasco's spirit pulsed in and out several times before disappearing altogether. Only then did Gunter ease his stance.

"That was odd." Jerry repeated the sentence when neither of his parents responded.

"Are you talking to us or the ghost?" Lori asked.

"Sorry, I was talking to you. Dr. Glasco is gone. There was something off about the guy."

Wayne glanced at Lori. "Off how?"

"Nothing I can put my finger on. Gunter felt it too. He stayed in between us the whole time."

Lori looked at the couch and pursed her lips. "That's because he's a good boy protecting his daddy."

Jerry pointed to the opposite side of the room. "He's over there, Mom, and we'd both appreciate it if you don't talk baby talk."

Wayne drew Jerry's attention. "So now what? How do you find the woman?"

"The easiest way? Ask my boss. If the woman is out there, Fred will find her."

"You said the ghost felt off. What if the woman doesn't want to be found?" Lori asked.

It was a legitimate question and could very well be why Dr. Glasco hadn't been able to track her down. "Good point. I'll tell Fred to be discreet."

Jerry walked to the back bedroom to place the call. He sat on the bed, and Gunter jumped up beside him.

"McNeal, how's the family treating you? Ready to come back to work yet?"

"I am working, kinda anyway. I'm looking for a woman by the name of Bernita Glasco who may live in The Villages. Her husband came to see me and asked if I could find her. I'm not sure where he fits into her life, so if you could keep this close, I'd appreciate it."

"Running her myself right now."

April was right: the man was the do-all king. "Do you sleep with your computer too?"

"Don't need to. They've implanted a chip in my brain that allows me to get information the moment I think of it."

Jerry chuckled. "Better watch who you tell that to. They might think you're serious."

"Who says I'm not?" Fred said solemnly.

Jerry knew Fred was messing with him, but it would explain how the guy was able to accomplish so much in such a short period of time.

"She's dead."

"Excuse me?"

"The woman you're looking for died about five years ago. You said her husband's looking for her?"

"Yep, he showed up here a few minutes ago asking about her."

"If I didn't know you better, I would say you're lying."

"Why's that?"

"Because he's dead too. The police labeled it a murder-suicide, with him being the murderer. They are both buried not too far from where you are in a cemetery in Homosassa. I'll send you the address. It looks to be just over an hour away. I would ask you if you need any help, but I think this one is over my head. I assure you, I don't say that too often."

"Keep saying that, and I'm going to ask for a raise."

Fred laughed a hearty laugh. "McNeal, I'll double your pay this very minute if you can tell me how much you make."

Jerry sighed into the phone.

Fred laughed even harder. "You, my friend, are a special breed. Anything else I can help you with?"

The thought of climbing back into the small car

to drive to the cemetery was less than appealing. "I'd like my Durango back."

"I'll see what I can find out."

"What, no waving your magic wand?"

"You seriously hate that car that much?"

It wasn't that he hated the car. He just missed his ride. "My mother's golf cart is bigger."

"I'll check on the status in the morning. Hey, McNeal?"

"That guy killed his wife. Do you have a way of protecting yourself if he gets violent?"

Jerry decided to have a little fun with the guy. "You think you can get me a few silver bullets?"

Fred took a moment to answer, and Jerry imagined him ordering some. "I thought silver bullets were for werewolves. Are you telling me they work on spirits too?"

"You've been watching too many zombie movies. You can't kill something that is already dead." Jerry frowned into the phone. "You do know werewolves aren't real, don't you?"

"Neither are ghost dogs, right?"

He's got you there, McNeal. "Touché."

"McNeal, coming from you, I'd believe just about anything. Seriously, though, what do you do if a ghost gets handsy?"

Jerry looked at Gunter and smiled. "I think that's why the dog is here."

"Good, you tell him to watch your six."

Jerry reached over and scratched Gunter behind the ear. "He always does."

Chapter Eleven

Jerry had just finished dressing when he heard a knock on his bedroom door. "Come in."

Lori entered, coffee cup in hand. "Sorry, just passing through. I wish I had thought to unlock the outer door last night. If I had, I could have gone around. I enjoy drinking my coffee on the porch. Want to join me?"

"Sure, let me grab a cup, and I'll be out."

Gunter looked from Jerry to Lori, then, deciding Jerry wasn't in danger, followed Lori outside.

The coffee pot was half empty. Jerry poured himself a cup and went to join his mom. He stood looking out at the swamp for a moment, then turned.

Gunter lowered the front of his body into a stretch, then followed with the rest of his body. Once down, he turned onto his side, let out an audible sigh, and closed his eyes. Jerry nodded to where the dog lay. “I think Gunter is in a sugar coma.”

His mother smiled. “Your father tells me you have a lady friend.”

Jerry took the seat next to her, turned it to face her, and matched Gunter’s sigh. “This has to be a new record. Normally, I can get through half a cup of coffee before you start drilling me on my life.”

Lori took a sip of coffee. “Would you feel more comfortable if we went for a drive for old times’ sake?”

“I was never comfortable during our drives. At least not when you started asking pointed questions.” Jerry chuckled. “Besides, the car I’m driving is lower to the ground, which would make it easier for me to roll out at a stop sign.”

“Oh, poo. Are you saying you never enjoyed any of our drives?”

“Maybe a little. You were pretty good at problem-solving, even if our discussions got a bit personal sometimes.”

A smile touched her lips. “I’m still pretty good at problem-solving or at least listening.”

Jerry took a sip of coffee. As the warm liquid slid down his throat, he realized that this wasn’t simply the check-in-the-box holiday visit he had tried to convince himself it was. It was part of the healing process his heart so desperately craved. He’d often spoken to his mother about things that were bothering him. While he and his father barely knew each other, his mother had always been there for him when he needed her. She'd listened to most of his problems, and even if she didn't have all the answers, she listened and made suggestions. Jerry searched his mind trying to decide where to start. "There is someone, and she's wonderful. I thought she might feel the same way, but then she told me there was no chemistry between us. But there is; I felt it. I think it's all a big misunderstanding, but what if I'm wrong?"

"Tell me about the misunderstanding," Lori said softly.

"It's a bit convoluted. The whole of it is a mutual friend told her I was hung up on someone else."

"Are you?" It was a simple question for which there wasn't a simple answer.

"I thought there could be someone else and, for a long time, wished there was. Holly was all I could think about until I met April. No, that's not true. At first, I was still hung up on Holly, but things changed as I began spending time with April. The more time I spent with her, the less I thought about Holly. And now all I can think about is how much I want to be with April."

"Have you ever actually told April this?"

Jerry shook his head. "No."

"Why not?" Lori held up her hand. "Think about it for a moment. I don't want a stock answer. I want you to dig deep and be honest with both of us.

You're a Marine. You know how to fight. Why haven't you fought for the woman you claim to care about so much?"

Dang, she's good. "Because I'm afraid."

"Afraid of what, Jerry? Rejection? What's the worst that can happen? Let me answer that. The worst thing that can happen is she tells you what she has already said: that she likes you as a friend and nothing more. If she says that, you deal with the rejection, dust off your ego, and move on. I know it is cliche, but there are plenty of fish in the sea, and you have a lot to offer a woman. I know I'm your mother and supposed to say that, but I also know it to be true. So let's take the rejection card off the table. Dig a little deeper, and tell your mom the truth. Tell me why you haven't told April you care about her?"

Jerry thought of the unopened e-mail from Holly still sitting in his inbox. "Because I'm not sure. My life has been a struggle of what-ifs. What if I can't save the person? What if this is not just a panic attack, and I'm actually having a heart attack? What if this is just a rebound thing, and I'm not actually in love with April? I'd rather be alone than hurt either April or Max."

"Max?"

At the mention of Max's name, Gunter lifted his head and disappeared.

"She's April's daughter and one amazing kid.

That's why I went to Michigan, on account of Max having the gift. She's the one that helped me with the serial killer case and a couple more. Max is so much better with this than I ever was at her age. She's smart and pretty. She looks just like April."

Lori smiled. "Jerry, I don't know anything about any of them, but your face doesn't lie. When you talk about April and Max, it lights up. I didn't see that when you mentioned Holly."

Jerry wanted so badly to believe her. "Maybe I should open the e-mail just to be sure."

Lori's brow creased. "E-mail?"

Jerry nodded. "From Holly. She sent it a while back, but I was afraid to open it."

"Jerry Carter McNeal, STOP IT."

Jerry raised an eyebrow.

"I swear I want to shake you and tell you to stop letting fear ruin your life. God help me, but sometimes I'm sorry you were born with the gift. Maybe you could have lived a normal life and stopped running away."

Jerry sighed. "If I had a nickel for every time I thought that way, I'd be rich."

Lori laughed. "I'm pretty sure you are the one person I know who has never had to worry about money."

That Jerry's brother Joseph had designated Jerry as beneficiary was no secret. Jerry had also significantly benefited from the wrongful death claim his uncle had filed on Joseph's behalf. "We all know why that is."

Lori narrowed her eyes. "You want to bring Joseph into this, fine. Let's talk about your brother. That boy was full of life until the moment he died."

"Yeah, and look where it got him."

Anger flashed in Lori's eyes. "Joseph made a mistake, Jerry. He didn't commit murder. He spray-painted graffiti on a government building. A childish decision that could have ruined his life, but he never let it get him down. He didn't run from things – he ran to them. Joseph never got to have a family, but you – Jerry, you deserve to be happy. If you want to honor your brother's memory, do this for him. Open that e-mail, decide what you want to do, and fight for it. But do it soon because I assure you this woe-is-me thing you've got going on at the moment isn't anything anyone will find sexy. Women want a man willing to fight for them." She winked. "How do you think your father and I ended up together?"

His mother was right. If his father had taken no for an answer, Jerry wouldn't be sitting here. "Okay, Mom."

Lori wagged a finger at him. "No, not okay. Promise me."

Jerry reached for her hand and kissed the back of it. "I promise." He went inside and pulled his computer bag from the closet. As he did, he saw a small box on the top shelf. He pulled it down, opened the top, and was met with the faces of the frogs he'd been collecting for his mother along his travels. *Dad must have stuck them in the box when he brought my bags inside.* Jerry placed the box on the bed, opened his computer bag, and powered up his laptop. It had been a while since he had turned it on, and it would be a few moments before it finished updating. He pulled out his phone to turn on the hotspot and saw it was still in airplane mode, which he had used to avoid disturbing his parents during the night. *That explains why it hasn't gone off today.* He switched off the restriction and was immediately slammed with text messages. Fred asking how ghost hunting was going and giving him details about Dr. and Mrs. Glasco. Two from Max apologizing for not texting him back sooner, saying she had been having so much fun with Chloe that she'd completely forgotten to respond. She sent a photo of her and Chloe making silly faces to make up for it. She'd sent another message when he didn't respond, asking if he were mad she hadn't answered.

Jerry smiled and typed a message. > *No, Max, I am not mad. I've just been busy with my parents.* He hit send.

Almost immediately, he received a reply. > *Cool, tell Gunter hi for me.*

Jerry > *Will do. Talk to you soon. Tell your mom I said hello.* Jerry started to erase the last, then hit send. *No guts, no glory, Marine.* Leaving his phone on the bed, he took the box to the porch and handed it to his mom.

"What's this?"

"Open it."

"Frogs! You know me so well." Lori's eyes sparkled as she dug into the box, drawing them out and inspecting each with loving hands. Her expression reminded him of April when he'd given her the teapot with the ladybugs. "They are adorable, Jerry. Thank you."

"No, it is I who should thank you."

"For being your mother?"

"No, just for being you."

"Oh, stop. Go on inside and do your thing before you make me cry."

The laptop was ready. Jerry signed into his e-mail account, scrolled until he found Holly's e-mail, and stared at the screen, his finger hovering over the message. His mother was right. It was time to know once and for all. He clicked on the e-mail. Instantly, Holly's words filled the screen.

Jerry, I hope this letter finds you well and hope you don't mind that I asked your sergeant to give me your contact information. By now, you probably know I no longer live in Pennsylvania. The accident scared me, and I promised myself if I lived, I would try to mend fences with my family. Whether or not my mother and I will ever see eye to eye is still to be determined, but regardless of that, I now live in a place where my daughter has people who care about her and can look after her if anything happens to me. An added plus, it rarely snows. My father and I moved back to Florida and will never again have to worry about getting trapped in a blizzard. Oh, I almost forgot to tell you they were able to save my leg. I will always be grateful to you for that and, most of all, for saving my life. I truly believe there are angels on earth and that you and the dog are two of them. I pray for you both each night and know that God has special plans for you. If anyone deserves to be happy, it is you.

If you ever find yourself in Destin, Florida, look me up. I still owe you a coffee date.

Holly- aka, your damsel in distress.

Ps. Did they ever find that dog?

Pss. Gracie wanted me to ask if your hair ever grew back.

Gracie had just finished chemo for childhood leukemia and had seen Jerry's shaved head and thought he, too, was sick. She'd touched his heart when she'd assured him the doctors would make him better.

Jerry ran a hand over his full head of hair. *I'm no angel. The dog, on the other hand …* Jerry looked for Gunter. Not seeing him, he wondered where he'd disappeared to, then pulled up Google map and checked the distance to Destin. *Five hours. If I left right now, I could be there by dinner. And say what,*

I was just passing by and decided to take you up on the coffee? Why not? He read through her e-mail once more. Casual, friendly, and nothing more. Still, he owed it to everyone involved, himself included, to be one hundred percent certain.

A whimper filled the air.

Gunter? Jerry turned in all directions but saw nothing but a small puddle on the tile. *What the heck is that?* He went to the kitchen, got a couple of paper towels, and bent to clean up the mess. He looked at the towels, saw they'd turned yellow, and brought them to his nose. *Urine? Gunter has never peed in the house before.* While he'd seen the dog go through the motions outside, he had never actually seen anything come of it. *It's a small puddle for such a big dog. Maybe he just got excited. Dogs do that all the time, according to TikTok.*

Jerry saw his mother coming and hurried back to the kitchen to dispose of the evidence. Lori had balked at the dog eating off her good dishes. He doubted she'd be happy with him using the bedroom as a urinal.

Lori met him in the hallway. "Are you okay?"

"Yes, why do you ask?"

"The e-mail."

"Oh, that. Yes, no great mystery. Holly was just thanking me for saving her life. Funny coincidence, she lives in Florida."

Lori arched an eyebrow. "Oh? So what are your

plans for the day?"

I'm going to Destin. Before Jerry could say the words out loud, the hairs on the back of his neck stood on end, letting him know they were no longer alone. He also knew whoever was visiting wasn't happy.

Lori's brow creased. "Are you okay, Jerry?"

Jerry placed a finger in front of his lips and turned when she nodded her understanding. He scanned the area and saw nothing. "Whoever's here, show yourself."

A mist hovered in near the front door. As it filled in, Dr. Glasco appeared. The spirit firmed his chin. "I'm looking for my wife."

"Your wife isn't here," Jerry informed him.

"Of course, she isn't. If she were, I would see her."

"No, I'm telling you your wife is dead."

Rage filled the man's face as he pointed a shaky finger at Jerry. "LIES!"

Gunter appeared wearing his police vest. His hackles were raised as he stood directly in front of the angry spirit and growled a ferocious warning.

The spirit faded in and out.

Jerry spoke, using his cop voice. "Are you aware that you also are dead?"

The energy surrounding the spirit winked in and out twice before finally disappearing.

Jerry rolled his neck and knelt, and Gunther

turned, whining and slathering Jerry with ghostly K-9 kisses. "Good boy, Gunter. You're one courageous dog."

"Jerry, I don't like ghosts coming into my home." Lori's voice cracked as she spoke.

Jerry stood and wrapped his arms around her. "I know, Mom. I promise to take care of this."

"How?"

"I'm going to go to his wife's grave. Once he sees she's dead, I think we can sort things out."

"Do you think it will work?"

"Don't worry. I may have doubts about many things, but this is one thing I'm good at." As the words spilled from his mouth, Jerry almost believed them.

Chapter Twelve

It had been a few days since Jerry had driven the Spark. While he had dreaded getting back inside, he'd spent so much time in it driving down from North Carolina that it almost felt comfortable. He was not ready to trade in his Durango, but he could deal with it, at least for now. The drive over to Homosassa wasn't bad. The route had him following FL-44, which for the most part, was rural with little to no traffic. It was a comfortable drive amidst horse farms and trees with moss draping from their branches. If someone were to show him a photo of the area and ask him to guess its location, Florida would be his guess. And yet, aside from the horse farms and trees not typical in the north, the area reminded him a lot of Michigan. He wondered if that was because a part of him felt he was betraying April and Max with his intended plan of visiting Holly after he got Dr. Glasco situated. Or perhaps it was simply because the terrain looked much like the part of Michigan where the two lived.

Jerry saw a bear-crossing sign. "Yo, dog, if alligators weren't bad enough, we also have to keep a lookout for bears."

Gunter took his comment to heart and stuck his head through the side window.

Jerry's cell rang. "Yes?"

"Are you there yet?"

"Almost."

"I really wish you would have taken your father with you. I don't like you doing this alone."

"This is what I always do, and I'm not alone, remember. I have Gunter with me." Gunter's tail thumped the seat, showing Jerry the dog was listening.

"I still wish you would have taken your father. The two of you need to spend some time together. You have a lot of catching up to do."

"I promise I will spend time with Dad before I leave."

"What if this visit you're going on turns out to be more?"

Jerry wasn't sure if she was referring to the spirit or Holly. "Most of my belongings are in your guest room. I will be back."

Lori sighed into the phone. "Okay, son. Just promise you'll be safe."

"I promise. Got to go. This thing I'm driving doesn't have hands-free."

"Jerry, you'll get a ticket for that in this state."

"I guess I'd better hang up, then. I'll call you before I head to Destin."

"Okay, Jerry. Oh, one more thing."

"Yeah, Mom?"

"I don't want to make a big deal of it because he saved your life, but I think Gunter piddled on the floor."

I cleaned that up. If Mom found one, that meant there was a second puddle. Jerry swallowed. "What makes you think that?"

She lowered her voice. "Your father stepped in something. When he lifted his foot, his sock was yellow. I fibbed and told him I'd been watering the plants, but I did that two days ago, and the plants were nowhere near the puddle. If you could talk to him about it…"

Jerry glanced at Gunter. "I will, Mom."

"Okay, Jerry, now hang up before you get in trouble with the police."

Jerry switched off the phone. "Yo, dog."

Gunter pulled his head through the glass.

"Are you feeling alright? Maybe I should ask Granny to take you to the ghost vet. Maybe you have a bladder infection or something." While Jerry knew the thought was absurd, he couldn't think of any other reason for the sudden onset of accidents.

Gunter lifted his lip and growled a soft growl.

Jerry nodded his understanding. "I don't like doctors either, but you can't keep urinating on the floor. It's not cool."

Gunter yawned a squeaky yawn and disappeared.

"I hope that means you're going to the vet!" Jerry yelled into the air.

***

Jerry didn't need a map to find the graves where Dr. and Mrs. Mortimer Glasco were buried. He knew what he was looking for, and he allowed the feeling to pull him into the cemetery, past a large fountain, and to the final resting place of the couple. That they were buried together spoke volumes. Had the couple not been together in later years, it was unlikely they would share a headstone. The headstone was larger than others around it, ornate without being ostentatious. Doing the math in his head, Jerry had the doctor at seventy-four while his wife had barely reached her seventy-second year. Gunter sniffed the base of the stone.

Jerry shook his head. "Sorry, fellow, I don't think you're going to find any extra bodies in these graves." *At least, I hope not.* Just thinking of the possibility caused the hairs on the back of his neck to stand on end. Gunter growled. Jerry realized thoughts of the Hash Mark Killer were not the cause of his tingle. Jerry turned to see Bernita Glasco standing behind him. Her white hair was perfectly curled and, except for the blue dress she currently wore, looked exactly as she had in the photo Fred had forwarded to him.

She smiled a wrinkled smile. “You’re him.”

“Him?”

“Jerry McNeal, the man with the dog.”

Jerry sighed. “Word travels fast.”

“Especially in the underground network.”

“Underground network?”

The spirit nodded toward her grave. “I was referring to the dead and buried. Oh, quit being such a prude, Jerry. You’re alive and well. You really need to lighten up. That, or I need to work on my material. Seriously, that was one of my best lines.”

“Sorry. I’m working on being more spontaneous.”

“It would do you well. Can you call off the dog? I don’t like the way he’s looking at me. He won’t attack me, will he? I’d hate to get a run in my hose.”

Jerry forced a smile. “No, ma’am. Gunter won’t bother you unless you bother me.”

“Oh, good, on account of they’re the only ones I have. I’d hate to go through eternity with holes in my stockings.”

This time, Jerry laughed.

“Okay, now that I have you loosened up, what can I do for you, tall, dark and handsome?”

Gunter yawned a squeaky yawn.

Mrs. Glasco sighed. “Wow, tough crowd.”

Jerry shook his head. "Don't mind the dog. He's used to being called the handsome one." Jerry paused for a moment. "Do you know why I'm here?"

Her smile returned. "I'd hoped it was to reunite me with my husband. I hope I'm not wrong."

Jerry rocked back on his heels. "You're not mad at him for killing you?"

Mrs. Glasco's jaw twitched. "My husband didn't kill me."

Jerry glanced at Gunter and then back to the woman. "The police report says otherwise."

"Then the police report is wrong." Mrs. Glasco began walking, and Jerry followed. Gunter moved to his left side and remained there as they strolled through the cemetery lawn. "I had Alzheimer's – just so you know, things like that don't follow you in death. Anyway, I knew I was slipping and made Morti promise not to let me be a burden on the family. He promised. A few years went by, and one day, everything was clear. I knew that I'd been lost in a fog, and that Morti had been taking care of me. As I said, it was a good day. We reminisced about all the things we'd done and enjoyed laughing and pretending everything was better, only we both knew it was only a matter of time before the curtain lowered again. I looked at him and reminded him of his promise.

"He went to the safe and brought out two syringes. I begged him to do it, but he couldn't. So I told him I would take the burden from him. He told me I had to do it quickly or it wouldn't be enough. I asked him why there were two syringes, and he said because he couldn't go on living without me." Mrs. Glasco gasped. "Our daughter! Oh, what must she think? You have to talk to her, Jerry. You mustn't let her think her father is a murderer. I've soiled his reputation." She placed a trembling hand to her mouth. "He lived such a good life, and his patients adored him. Lord have mercy, what have I done?"

Doctor Glasco appeared in front of them. Gunter went on alert, then stood down when the doctor took his wife in his arms. Holding her close, he soothed her worries. "There, there, Lovey. You did nothing wrong. I would have done it eventually – I was just working up the courage to let you go. You had enough for the both of us and have nothing to be sorry for."

"I've missed you, Morti. Where have you been?"

"I was looking for you, my love, and would have gladly spent eternity doing so. Even in death, I wanted nothing more than to be with the woman I love. I was prepared to search for you forever."

"I'm here now, Morti." She pulled away from him. "Tell Jerry he needs to speak with Crissy. This must all be so hard on her. She can't go through the rest of her life thinking you killed me."

Dr. Glasco turned to Jerry, his energy calm now that he'd found what he'd been searching for. The spirit hadn't been angry, as Jerry had believed. He'd been desperate – willing to fight for the woman he loved even in death. "Please, won't you help us?"

Jerry pulled out his notebook. "Do you know how I can get in touch with your daughter?"

Mrs. Glasco smiled. "Her name is Crissy Brown. She lives in Lady Lake, Florida. It's not that far."

Jerry nodded. "I know where it is." Actually, he knew exactly where it was – an hour and nine minutes in the opposite direction he'd planned on going and ten minutes from where his parents lived.

Dr. Glasco scrunched his face. "Unless something's changed, you'll find her at the American Legion Post 347. She and her husband Matt are members. Chrissy volunteers there a lot. I wish I had a picture of her to show you."

Jerry shook his head. "Not necessary. Now that I know who I'm looking for, I'll be able to find her. I may need you both to show up if I need help convincing her."

"She won't be able to see us. Oh, Morti, I knew we should have called her that day."

"There, there, Lovey, it will be alright. Just you wait and see."

"She won't need to see you as long as you are there to answer questions."

"You're going there tonight, aren't you?"

Jerry placed his notebook back in his pocket and managed a smile. "Yes, ma'am. I'll stop by in a couple of hours, and we can all chat."

"Thank you, Jerry. I knew we could count on you." They both disappeared before he had a chance to reply. Jerry started for his car and motioned for Gunter to follow. "Looks like we're not going to the beach after all."

Gunter woofed, dipped into a playful bow, and then he, too, disappeared.

Jerry scratched his head. *Where do you keep running off to, dog?* He pulled out his cell phone and dialed his dad's number as he started for his car. When Wayne didn't answer, he dialed his mom's cell.

"Jerry? I've been beside myself with worry. Is everything alright?"

"Everything's fine, Mom."

"And the ghost?"

"I'm still working on it."

"Oh."

"Don't worry. Everything is going to be okay. Dr. Glasco isn't going to come by the house anymore. It was all a misunderstanding."

"You said he murdered his wife. It must have been one heck of a misunderstanding."

Jerry chuckled. "I promise to fill you in on all the details when I get back. I tried calling Dad, but he didn't answer."

She laughed. "He's probably got the volume down. He does it all the time. He went to the store to pick up something for tomorrow's dinner. You'll be back in time, won't you?"

Jerry's mouth watered. "You're cooking Thanksgiving dinner?"

"Yes, we had reservations at Coastal Del Mar, but I canceled them. If your father wants a home-cooked meal, I will give him a Thanksgiving feast he won't soon forget. Tell me you'll be here."

"Will there be stuffing?"

"Of course. What would Thanksgiving be without stuffing?"

"I'll be there."

"What about that other thing you were going to look into?"

"I've decided it can wait until after the holiday."

"But you're still going?"

"Yes, Mom, I'm going to go. Just not today. Hey, do you mind if I take Pop out for a beer tonight?"

"Mind? I'd love it. The man's been underfoot all day. Why, I had to invent a reason to send him to the store. He was about to pester me to death, pulling up recipes on his phone and acting like I don't know anything about cooking. I may not have cooked a meal in a while, but I still know my way around the kitchen. Maybe you should make that several beers. If he has a hangover in the morning, he will stay out of my way."

Jerry laughed. "Don't worry about Dad. I'll keep him out of your hair." A car pulled out in front of him. Jerry laid on the horn and wanted to crawl under a rock as the meek noise croaked from under the hood.

"Jerry Carter McNeal, are you driving and talking with a phone in your hand?"

He started to lie and tell her he had his phone on speaker. "Yes, ma'am."

The phone went silent. "How do you like that? My own mother hung up on me." Jerry laughed and looked to the seat where Gunter usually sat, disappointed not to see him sitting there.

Chapter Thirteen

Wayne was standing by the front door when Jerry approached. His father pointed a thumb behind him. “You don’t want to go in there.”

Jerry peeked around him and saw his mother standing at the stove. “Problem?”

Wayne lowered his voice to keep her from hearing. “Your mother is cooking.”

Jerry frowned and scratched his head. “I didn’t think dinner was until tomorrow.”

“It’s not. That’s the problem. She sent me to the store to get a turkey, and everything they had was frozen. I went to three stores before I finally picked up a ham. But you know your mother, it’s not Thanksgiving without a turkey. So now, the woman’s making enough food to feed a small army. Seriously, Jerry, I think she plans on feeding everyone on the street.”

Jerry laughed. "Maybe I shouldn't have told her you missed her cooking."

"I'm not going to have a chance to miss it. At the rate she's going, there'll be enough leftovers to eat for a month. She thinks she's doing me a favor by sending me out for a beer. I didn't have the heart to tell her she's driving me to drink with all her clanging and banging. I've seen her cook before, Jerry. This..." Wayne waved a hand. "She's acting like that guy on TV that does all the cooking and yells at people. She was looking for a recipe, so I tried to be helpful by finding one on my phone. That look she gave me – I'm telling you, I think the woman's possessed."

Jerry stared at his mother through the doorway, weighing his father's accusations. "No, Pop, she's not possessed. She's just doing what she always does and trying to make everything perfect."

Wayne's shoulders relaxed. "Are you sure, son?"

"Yeah, Pop. I'm sure. We just need to give her space to do her thing." Jerry started back toward the car.

"She said you want a beer. There are a few good places in the square," Wayne said as he followed.

Jerry shook his head. "I thought we'd go over to the legion hall."

"That works too. Wait 'til you see this place. It's great. It is the largest American Legion Post in the world. We've got over sixty-seven hundred members."

"You're a member?"

"Yep, a lifetime member. Got my laminated card to prove it." Wayne stared at him over the roof of the car. "Want me to drive?"

Jerry smiled. "Not unless you're afraid to be seen in a teal roller skate. Besides, Mom said I'm supposed to get you drunk. I'd hate to have to wrestle you for your keys."

"What if you get drunk?" Wayne asked, ducking inside.

Jerry lowered into the driver's seat. "Not going to happen. I know my limit."

"Which is?" Wayne asked, pulling his seatbelt around.

"Six." Jerry laughed when his father whipped his head toward him. "Relax, Pop, I'm kidding. I never have more than two when I know I'm going to be driving."

"You had me worried there for a moment, son. First your mother and now you – I was starting to think I was in another dimension."

Jerry took a left onto Juarez Place. After a short distance, he turned left onto Juarez Way, then took another left onto San Marino Drive.

Wayne cleared his throat.

Jerry glanced at the man. "Problem, Pop?"

"No. Just wondering where you get your sense of direction from. It's sure not from me or your mother."

Jerry followed the pull and turned left onto Morse Boulevard. "Am I going the wrong way?"

"Nope, that's the point. It's like you've been there before."

Jerry grinned. "Nope. Just letting the pull guide me."

"So, what, is your brain like an internal Alexa where you say, 'I think I'll have a beer. Brain, take me to the American Legion post 347'?"

Jerry's grin turned into a chuckle. "Not quite. The truth of it is I'm working on a case. I know who I'm going to see, and that knowledge is what is pulling me to where I need to go."

"You're working? So, I'm like your wingman?"

"Yep." Jerry heard a growl and looked in the rearview mirror to see Gunter had returned. He winked at the dog. Gunter smiled a K-9 smile.

Wayne drummed his fingers together. Jerry knew the gesture well. "What's on your mind, Pop?"

"You seemed surprised I'm a member of the legion. I know being stationed on a lake in Kentucky with the Coast Guard doesn't sound like much compared to what you did in the Marines, but I did my time."

Jerry cocked an eyebrow. "I've never thought otherwise."

"You sounded surprised."

Jerry suddenly realized where he got his self-doubt from. It was also clear he needed to talk to his father more, as there was so much they needed to learn about each other. "I was surprised that Mom never mentioned it. Not that you are a member. Why the sudden attitude?"

Wayne sighed. "Sorry. I suppose I did come across as a jerk. I guess I'm the one with the attitude. Maybe, deep down, I do feel guilty when I hear some of the guys tell their war stories, and all I can contribute is I had to fight off water moccasins and issue drunk-driving tickets to intoxicated boaters. Heck, even Uncle Marvin has better war stories than me."

Jerry resisted the urge to roll his eyes. While he had mended fences with his uncle, a part of him was still living with his past ill-will toward the man. "We both know Uncle Marvin was never in the service."

"That's the point. The guy never served a day in his life and still has better stories."

"Between you and me, Marvin's lucky no one ever called him on it. Real veterans don't take stolen valor too lightly." Jerry pulled into the parking lot. "There are a lot of motorcycles."

"Most likely, all members of the American Legion Riders. They are huge in the area. They do a lot of fundraising and provide escorts for funerals. I wanted to join, but your mother knows how clumsy I am and vetoed my getting a Harley."

Jerry put the car in park and pulled the key from

the ignition. "I saw a bunch of those three-wheeled Spyders while I was in Homosassa. They seem pretty popular and look safe. Maybe Mom would agree to one of those."

Wayne closed the door. "That's an idea. You can help me talk her into it."

Jerry laughed and shook his head as he waited for Gunter to jump out. "Sorry, Pop. You're on your own with this one. You get into a wreck, and Mom would never forgive me. Hey, whatever happened to the fancy golf cart you were getting?"

"It's hiding in Gertie's garage. I suppose your mom's saving it for Christmas."

"Gertie told you it's there?"

Wayne shook his head as they walked toward the building. "Nope, I saw the truck deliver it. Since Gertie has never mentioned it, I'm assuming it's the one your mom ordered."

Jerry held the door open for his dad and followed him inside. Wayne walked straight to the bar and ordered a Budweiser, then looked at Jerry.

"Same."

The bartender nodded. Gunter jumped up, placing his front feet on the bar, sniffing the bartender as he turned away. The man turned, frowned, then rolled his neck as he walked away.

Jerry looked around the room. The area above the bar was decorated with liquor bottles. The building's interior was bright with recessed lighting.

Several televisions were spread about the light-colored room. The rest of the walls were lined with military plaques and photos.

Wayne followed Jerry's gaze. "I told you it was a nice place."

"Very nice," Jerry agreed.

"Hey, there's an empty table. We'd better grab it before someone gets it."

Actually, the table wasn't empty. Dr. Glasco and his wife were sitting there, which probably explained why no one else had claimed it. Mrs. Glasco raised her hand to get his attention. Jerry smiled as he reached for his wallet.

Wayne waved him off as the bartender set their beers on the bar. "I've got this, son. Secure the table, Marine."

"Commencing to secure the table, aye." Jerry laughed.

Gunter followed as he took his glass to the table and left his father to pay. Several people at a nearby table gaped at him when he sat. Gunter made his way under the table, positioning himself to watch Jerry's back.

"We didn't have anything better to do, so we thought we'd save you a table. We've been here for over an hour shooing people away." Mrs. Glasco snickered. "Haunting is much more fun with my Morti here."

That explains all the bewildered looks. Jerry

resisted the urge to smile as he scanned the room. His gaze settled on a brunette with a purple streak in her hair talking to a couple at a table on the other side of the room. The woman was pregnant and looked a couple of years older than him. Though she smiled, she appeared surrounded by an aura of sadness. Jerry knew why and hoped he could help – provided he would be able to get her to agree to speak with him.

Mrs. Glasco grabbed hold of her husband's arm. "He's good. We didn't even have to point her out."

Jerry took a drink of his Bud and stared at the woman as he swallowed.

"Boy, we lucked out getting a table," Wayne said, joining him.

"Luck had little to do with it," Jerry replied without looking.

"How's that?" Wayne asked.

"We have company. Dr. Mortimer Glasco and his wife."

Wayne leaned closer to Jerry. "We're having beers with a murderer and the woman he killed?"

"It wasn't murder. I'm going to try and clear it up," Jerry told him, still watching the woman.

"How?" Though his father had asked the question aloud, Dr. and Mrs. Glasco echoed the question to his subconscious.

Jerry sighed as he turned to face them all. "I haven't a clue. But that's part of the job – going with the flow and letting my intuition guide me in the right direction."

Wayne blinked his confusion. "What do you need me to do?"

"Honestly, Dad, I'm better off working alone." A growl drifted up from below the table. "Oh, for Pete's sake. We – Gunter and I – prefer working as a team."

"We're not leaving until Chrissy knows the truth," Dr. Glasco said firmly.

Jerry looked at the doctor. "I don't want you to leave. I just need you to let me work."

"Okay, Jerry. I'll sit here and drink my beer. I might need another, though, because this one seems to be making me nervous."

Jerry turned, saw that Chrissy's chair was empty, and turned again. "Where'd she go?"

Wayne blinked his confusion. "Where'd who go?"

And this was why he preferred to work alone. Jerry closed his eyes and concentrated on Chrissy. "Hang on a minute, Pop." Jerry stood and followed the pull, and met the woman as she was coming out of the ladies' room.

Her eyes widened, and then recovered. "If you're looking for a dance partner, you're out of luck. My ankles are swollen and my feet hurt."

For a moment, Jerry thought she knew who he was.

"You've been staring at me since you came in." She smiled. "Just kidding, my friends told me, and I snuck a peek at you when you weren't looking. So, let me guess, you have a thing for pregnant women." She cupped her hands around her stomach, flashed her wedding ring, and laughed. "Sorry, tall, dark, and handsome, you're cute, but I'm afraid you're too late."

Jerry tried to keep a straight face, but he couldn't. Chrissy reminded him so much of her mother, he couldn't resist smiling.

Chrissy arched an eyebrow. "I wish all my rejections went this well."

"I was just thinking how much you remind me of your mother."

The color drained from her face. "You knew my mother?"

Easy, Jerry, one scream, and every guy in the place will be on top of you. "I did. Would you care to join me at my table for a few moments? I would love to talk to you about her."

"If this is some kind of creepy pick-up line, you'll be sorry."

Jerry waved a hand around the room. "I think you're safe." He nodded to his table. "Besides, I wouldn't make a move on you with my dad sitting at the table."

"Okay, let me get my water, and I'll join you. But just to be clear, I'm telling my friends if they see me leaving with you, to call the police."

Jerry instantly thought of Patty and the other victims of the Hash Mark Killer. If only they'd had the same forethought, maybe some of them would have gotten away. "You're a smart woman, Chrissy."

"I'm also very pregnant and need to get off my feet. I'll join you in a moment."

Jerry looked at Gunter. "Ready to do this?"

Gunter barked and wagged his tail.

"Yeah, that makes one of us." Jerry saw a man watching and realized it looked like he was talking to himself. He smiled a sheepish grin and joined his father at the table.

"Did you settle things?" Wayne asked as he sat.

"No, Pop, just getting started."

"Sounds like we're both going to need another beer."

"Dad, I need you to do me a favor."

"Yeah, Jerry?"

"That woman I was just talking to is coming over for a chat. I'm going to be telling her some things. I want you to pretend you've heard it all before and save any questions until after we're done. She's coming."

Wayne looked around him, then sat back in his chair and lifted his glass. "If I didn't know better, I'd say you have eyes in the back of your head."

"Trust me, I've checked." Both Jerry and Wayne

stood. Jerry pulled out Chrissy's chair and waited for her to sit before returning to his seat. Gunter moved beside her without being told and laid his head in the woman's lap.

Instantly, the energy around the woman calmed. She took the cap off her water bottle and took a drink. Replacing the cap, she spoke. "So, how'd you know my mother?"

Jerry smiled to appear calmer than he was. He pulled his wallet from his pants and laid a business card and badge in front of her.

"Jerry McNeal. You're him!" she said, repeating her earlier comment. "The guy with the ghost dog. People were talking about you, but I thought it was all a joke."

Jerry sighed. "If it is, it's not very funny."

Gunter bared his teeth.

"What I mean is I take my job very seriously."

"Okay, so what do you want from me?"

"I'm going to tell you some things, and I need you to hear me out."

"I won't run screaming from the table if that's what you're saying."

"She always was a sharp one." Mrs. Glasco beamed.

"Your father visited me yesterday and asked for help finding your mother."

"Did he tell you he killed her?"

Mrs. Glasco touched him on the arm. "Jerry, tell

her he didn't do it."

Jerry leaned forward and placed his hands on the table. "Your mother wants me to tell you your father didn't kill her."

Chrissy laughed. "Sorry. I don't know what I expected, but that wasn't it."

Jerry wasn't sure if she was referring to the supposed murder or saying that her mother was there. "I've been doing this long enough to know how far-fetched this sounds. I assure you I'm telling the truth. Your mother had Alzheimer's disease."

"That's no big secret, Mr. McNeal. Neither is the fact that he killed her, then killed himself."

"I know that's what you think happened. But your mother said your father couldn't do it, so she did it herself."

"You are saying she injected herself with a lethal dose of something that stopped her heart."

"Bupivacaine," Dr. Glasco told him. Jerry repeated his words.

"That could have been a lucky guess."

"It could have been, but it wasn't."

Chrissy's lips trembled. "Why?"

Mrs. Glasco tugged at his arm. "I need to speak to her."

"Your mother wants to talk to you. She will tell me what to say, and I'll repeat it."

"How do I know you're not trying to scam me?"

"Because I won't ask for anything in return, and

she will make sure you know it's her."

"Your father promised me," her mother said gently. She kept talking, and Jerry repeated her words. "We knew I was getting worse, and I asked him to do it for me. No, not for me, but because I'd seen too many people go through it and didn't want to put your father through the heartache. Only, he didn't keep his promise. I would come out of the fog and beg him to set me free. Then, one day, the fog was gone, and I remembered. Your father and I went to Crumps Landing and sat at a table overlooking the water. We ordered a bucket of beer and seafood gumbo. As we ate, we talked about the time we took you to Florida Cracker Kitchen, and we each ordered a cinnamon roll. Your eyes were as round as saucers when you saw the size of it. I couldn't finish mine, but you, you matched your father bite for bite. And the time when you were little, and we took you to Weeki Wachee Springs so you could see the mermaids. We were supposed to make a day of it, but it started to storm, and they closed the park. You were so upset that we went back the next day."

Tears streamed down Chrissy's face. "But if you remembered all of that, maybe you were getting better. You should have waited to see."

"No, I wasn't getting better, Chrissy. I was just having a good day. We ate so much, and yet, after dinner, your father took me to the Twistee Treat soft serve to put the fire out from the gumbo."

At the mention of ice cream, Gunter lifted his head and licked his lips.

"I'm sorry we didn't leave a note. I was so determined to spare your father the pain of seeing me live in a world where I did not know him that I never stopped to think what it would do to him. Please forgive me."

"Us." Dr. Glasco placed his hand on Chrissy's. "Please forgive us for leaving you alone."

***

Jerry's shoulders sagged so much, he thought his knuckles would drag on the ground. He'd forgotten to protect himself, and his mistake had drained him of his energy. He reached into his pocket and pulled out the keys.

Wayne took them from him. "I'll drive, son."

"You good, Pop?"

Wayne smiled. "I never finished my second beer. Is this what you've been doing all these years?"

Jerry waited for Gunter to jump into the backseat, then settled into the passenger seat. "Some of it. But this…this part is new."

Wayne pulled on his seatbelt and started the car. He sat staring out the front window. "All those wasted years. I didn't know."

Jerry closed his eyes. "How could you? I never let you in."

"That thing you did in there, it was incredible. I felt like I was actually listening to the mother speak.

I want you to know I'm proud of you, son."

As Wayne drove from the parking lot, Jerry turned his head toward the side window and brushed away his tears.

Chapter Fourteen

Jerry's phone dinged. He hurried to squelch the volume and saw it was after eleven. Voices drifted through the bedroom door. Jerry looked for Gunter, but the dog wasn't in the room. Jerry checked his phone, saw he had a message from April, and hurried to open it. *>Happy Thanksgiving. Go Lions.*

Jerry started to text back to make a dig about her choice of teams and stopped. He backspaced and wrote, *>Maybe this will be their year*. He hit send and realized he hadn't wished her a Happy Thanksgiving and started to type a second message. Erasing what he'd just written, he pressed to make the call.

"Hello, Mr. McNeal. Why are you bothering us on a holiday?"

Jerry's heart sank.

"What? Fine, hang on. Hi, Jerry, sorry about that.

I left my phone on the table, and my friend Carrie answered for me. I don't know what she said to you, but she said to tell you she was kidding."

Instantly, Jerry relaxed. "She told me that you are madly in love with me." The comment was met with silence. "April, are you there? I was kidding."

"Oh." A nervous giggle floated through the phone. "How are things going with your parents?"

"Good. Really good," Jerry answered truthfully. "Dad and I went out and had a beer last night."

"Good for you. I'm more of a wine person myself. I'm glad the two of you are getting along so well."

"Me too. I'm glad I made the trip. We have a lot of lost years to catch up on. Not that I plan on staying much longer, but I know I'll call him a lot more."

"I'm glad things are working out for you. You deserve to be happy, Jerry. I'm afraid it would take more than a few beers to fix my family." April laughed. "That's right!"

"What's right?"

"Carrie reminded me that she is our family." Another laugh. "She also reminded me I promised to peel potatoes. I guess that's my hint she needs help. Tell your mom and dad I said hello. I know I haven't met them, but you've talked about them enough that I feel like I already know them. I'm sure Max will check in with you a bit later. Take care, Jerry."

"I will. You have a happy Thanksgiving." Jerry

held on to the phone until the screen went dark. He had just finished showering and getting dressed when he heard his mother scream. He grabbed his pistol from the top of the dresser and opened the bedroom door, cautiously scanning the living area. Not seeing anything amiss, his eyes trailed to the kitchen.

His mother stood in the middle of the floor, holding the broom over her head. She saw him and looked down. Jerry eased his way around the island, pausing when he saw his father crawling around the floor holding a butcher knife.

Jerry placed the pistol into his waistband. "Tell me this is a new kind of party game."

Lori lowered the broom. "It most certainly is not. I saw a rat!"

Jerry looked around the room. "Are you sure?"

Wayne waited until Lori wasn't looking and shook his head.

"I saw that!"

"What's with this family? Everyone has eyes in the back of their head except me. I'm telling you, there isn't a mouse. If there were, there would be a hole."

"It wasn't a mouse. It was a rat. Rats are bigger, and this one was huge. I saw it out of the corner of my eye." Lori gasped. "Do you think that's what is peeing on the floor?"

Jerry wanted to say no, but it made more sense

than to think Gunter had suddenly lost control of his bladder. Speaking of the dog, Jerry was surprised he wasn't here. His mother's scream had sounded real enough to make him bring his gun. Gunter should have picked up on that. "Have you seen Gunter?"

Wayne looked over his shoulder. "You're kidding, right?"

Jerry laughed a nervous laugh. "Yeah, I guess I am. It's just I'm surprised he didn't come when Mom screamed."

Wayne grabbed hold of a dining room chair, pulled himself up to standing, and handed Lori the knife. "That's it. I think the dog was here all along, heard your mother scream, and disposed of the rat himself."

Jerry started to tell his father that was absurd. But the man was now staring at him as if to say, *If you know what's good for you, you'll agree*. Jerry sniffed the air, his mouth watering as he tried to sort out the combination of smells, the most prominent of which was his mother's homemade stuffing. He nodded. "You know, I bet you're right."

Lori studied his face for a moment before walking to the counter and placing the knife in the sink. "Well, good riddance to that nasty varmint. I can still see his beady little eyes and long black tail."

While Jerry wasn't convinced Gunter had carried the rodent away, he was sure that his mother was telling the truth, or at least thought she was. He started for the garage.

"Where are you going?" Lori asked.

"I'm going to take a walk around the house to see if I can find out how the mouse got in."

"Rat, Jerry. I know I only saw it for a second out of the corner of my eye, but it was much too big to be a mouse." She handed him the broom. "Here, take this with you. When you're done, leave it in the garage. And take your father with you."

"Do you think she really saw a mouse?" Wayne asked the moment he closed the door.

"She believes she saw something." Jerry started around the house, checking the area around the foundation as they walked. "She's been under a lot of stress with the dinner."

"You've got that right. She woke me at five this morning crying because you wouldn't get your turkey."

Jerry sighed. "I promise to give her plenty of warning the next time I decide to visit."

Wayne clamped him on the shoulder. "It wouldn't have mattered. She would still be trying to cook you a perfect meal."

"What are you two looking for?"

They turned to see Sandy standing behind them.

Wayne took the lead. "Lori thought she saw a rat. She'd been upset, so we are humoring her by checking around the house to make sure there aren't any holes."

"A rat? I've been living here for fifteen years and haven't had any in the house. I guess it could have come in from the swamp. Is she sure it was a rat? Did she get a good look at him?"

Jerry shook his head. "No, she saw it out of the corner of her eye."

Sandy smiled. "Maybe it was a ghost. The woman who used to live here had a cat. After Sheba – that was the cat's name – died, Dotty used to swear she would see her out of the corner of her eye."

Wayne turned to him. "Have you seen a ghost cat, Jerry?"

"No, but it's as good an explanation as anything else I've heard."

"Why is Lori upset?"

Jerry glanced at Wayne. "Because she thought she saw a rat."

"No, you said she'd been upset, and that was why you are humoring her."

Wayne nodded his understanding. "Because the turkeys are frozen."

"Turkey? I thought she said you guys had reservations for Thanksgiving dinner."

"We did. Lori canceled them. She wanted to cook Jerry a homecooked Thanksgiving dinner. I went to the store yesterday, and all the turkeys they had left were frozen. I bought a ham, but you know Lori needs everything to be perfect. To make up for it, she spent yesterday prepping every dish she could think of and has been in the kitchen since a little after five this morning."

Jerry suddenly felt incredibly guilty about sleeping in.

Sandy looked at Jerry and made a noise. "You should have called."

Jerry sighed. "Yes, ma'am. I assure you if I could turn back time, I would give my mother adequate warning."

Sandy snapped her fingers. "What if we can give your mother her turkey?"

"I'd say that would be great. What do you have in mind?"

The woman smiled. "You said she's made extra, right?"

Wayne sighed. "I've never seen so much food."

"Gertie and I were planning on eating together. I have a turkey breast in the oven. We didn't want to go to a lot of trouble, so we were going to fix some instant potatoes, throw in some rolls, and call it a day. We could share our bird unless you think we'd be intruding on your family time."

Jerry didn't want to speak for his mother. "I think it would be a great idea. What do you think, Pop?"

"I think your mother would never forgive herself if she found out her friends ate instant potatoes on Thanksgiving Day."

Sandy clapped her hands together. "Oh, good. I'll call Gertie and let her know."

Wayne waited until she was out of earshot before talking. “Now, when we go inside, I want you to wait a bit and then tell your mother you see the ghost of the cat.”

“I can’t lie to her like that, Pop.”

“Yes, you can, and you will. That woman has spent two days standing over that stove for you. If she thinks there is even the slightest possibility of a rat inside, she will never have another decent night’s sleep in that house. Eventually, she will want to put it on the market. Your mother loves this house, Jerry. Don’t take that away from her because you can’t tell a little white lie.”

His father was right. The ghost of a cat would have to be better than living with a rodent. Besides, for all he knew, Gunter really could have saved the day by disposing of the thing. It would explain the dog’s absence. “Okay, Dad. I’ll tell her I see a cat.”

Lori was standing at the stove stirring the potatoes when they went back inside.

“We are having company for dinner,” Wayne announced as he stepped inside.

Lori’s hand flew to her head, patting at her hair. “Company?”

“Don’t you worry, love. You look wonderful. Besides, it is only Gertie and Sandy. We saw Sandy outside. The poor dear was talking about going in the house to fix instant potatoes.”

Lori’s eyes rounded. “They’re having instant

potatoes for Thanksgiving dinner?"

Wayne shook his head. "Not anymore. I told her you would be beside yourself if you found out she and Gertie had not eaten a proper Thanksgiving dinner. You know what she said?"

"No."

"Why, she asked what she was supposed to do with the turkey breast she has in the oven."

Lori's eyes lit up. "What did you tell her?"

"I told her to bring it over here, of course."

Lori placed her palms together and looked at the ceiling.

Wayne caught Jerry's attention.

Jerry let out an exaggerated gasp.

Lori jumped. "What's wrong? Did you see the rat? We can't have house guests if there's a rat!"

Jerry pointed to the corner. "Nope, not a rat, a cat. Black with a long tail, just like you described. You mean to tell me you don't see it?"

Wayne leaned toward the spot where Jerry had pointed. "I don't see anything. Do you, my dear?"

"No. Are you sure it's a cat? Maybe you just see a shadow."

Jerry walked to the corner, bent, and pretended to pick up the feline. "She's a ghost."

For a moment, Jerry thought he'd overplayed his hand, as his mother didn't look too convinced.

Finally, Lori firmed her chin. "I guess if our son can live with a ghost dog, we can live with a ghost cat. But you'll need to talk to her, Jerry."

Jerry bent and lowered the nonexistent cat. "Talk to her?"

"Yes, tell her she can stay, but I will not tolerate her tinkling on the floor. You know how bad cat urine is. You can never get rid of that smell. Now, out of my kitchen so I can get everything ready for our company."

***

Jerry lay on the couch, too full to move, as he listened to the easy conversation between his parents on the other side of the room. Wayne stood drying the dishes his mother insisted on washing since they wouldn't all fit in the dishwasher. "It was an incredible meal, Lori. You should be proud of your hard work. Everyone got fed and even went home with leftovers."

"Don't you patronize me, Wayne McNeal. I know what you did."

"What did I do?"

"Sandy told me you told her I was upset about not having a turkey."

"What if I did? Is it a crime to want the woman I love to be happy?"

"No." They grew quiet, and Jerry knew they had kissed. His heart filled, and he sighed.

"You okay, Jerry?" Lori asked, coming into the living area.

"I'm good, Mom. Are you sure you don't need

any help?"

"No, your father always helps me with the holiday dishes. I'll be right back. I have to put these linens in the hamper."

A few seconds later, his mother returned. As she walked into the room, Jerry could feel the startled energy surrounding her. He was up in an instant. "Mom? What's the matter?"

Her face was pale. For a moment, Jerry thought she was going to pass out. She lifted her arm, pointing in the direction she'd just come. Jerry started down the hall, smiling his relief when he saw Gunter standing in the doorway to his room. *Wait, had his mother seen the dog?*

He was just about to ask, when a tiny black German Shepherd puppy emerged from within the shadows of the room. The pup trotted into the hall, lowered, and left a small puddle on the floor.

Join Jerry McNeal and his ghostly K-9 partner as they put their gifts to good use in:

Special Delivery

Book 12 in the Jerry McNeal series.

Available January 20, 2023 on Amazon Kindle:

Also, ***Spirit of Deadwood***, a full-length Jerry McNeal novel, will be available March, 2023!

Please help me by leaving a review!

About the Author

Sherry A. Burton writes in multiple genres and has won numerous awards for her books. Sherry's awards include the coveted Charles Loring Brace Award, for historical accuracy within her historical fiction series, The Orphan Train Saga. Sherry is a member of the National Orphan Train Society, presents lectures on the history of the orphan trains, and is listed on the NOTC Speaker's Bureau as an approved speaker.

Originally from Kentucky, Sherry and her Retired Navy Husband now call Michigan home. Sherry enjoys traveling and spending time with her husband of more than forty years.